I0672910

# MIKASA
## BLURRED LINES: BOOK 1
## COCOA BROWN

PRETTY PURSE MEDIA

This book is a work  of fiction. Names, characters, places, and incidents are products of the author's imagination or are used fictitiously. Any resemblance to actual events or locales or persons, living or dead are entirely coincidental.

PRETTY PURSE MEDIA

ISBN: 979-8-9895674-0-9

Pretty Purse Media paperback printing 2024

Printed in the U.S.A.

# MAIN CHARACTERS

**Mikasa Jones** - the main character

**Brandon Williams** - Mikasa Jones' first cousin on her mothers' side

Patti Jones - Mikasa's Mother

Darius Jones - Mikasa's Father

Sara Williams - Mikasa's Aunt/Patti's only sister

Pooch (Darius) Jackson - Mikasa's love interest

# PROLOGUE

The room is cool and smells incredible from the almond soufflé crème that Mikasa rubbed gently on her skin. She was lying on her bed, nestled under a beautiful chocolate goose down comforter, smiling in her sleep, dreaming about him. In her mind was a vision of his smooth brown skin. He was handsome and built like the Rock. She could see him from a distance watching her, longing to talk to and get next to her. He was slowly approaching her. He walked right up to her and instantly, nothing else mattered. He walked forward quickly and kissed her. He was gentle and strong, holding her, touching her cheek, caressing her thigh…

Mikasa was stirring now. Her eyelids were heavy; she was still so drowsy.

She softly murmured, "That felt so real, umm."

Something moved in the room. Someone was breathing, rhythmic and controlled. Mikasa laid her head back on the pillow and sighed. She didn't realize it, but Brandon was right behind her, in her bed trying his best to remain still, but he was poking her now. He had been in the room for the past thirty minutes, and in her bed for about ten minutes. He was doing everything that he could to slow and readjust his breathing; trying to relax his body so that he did not awaken her. But just as she was drifting back to sleep, she felt it, something brushing against the back of her thigh.

'Pooch,' she mumbled. She felt a hand on her thigh. 'How did you get in here?' She backed into his embrace as he kissed her ear, and then she tensed up immediately. She turned around, horrified. She knew Pooch's' lips and these were not them. In the shadowy darkness, she recognized her cousin Brandon. Immediately she was enraged.

'What the hell are you doing in my room, and why are you in my bed, BRANDONNNN!?' Mikasa yelled, as she jumped up pushing him in the chest, and back towards her door all at once.

"Where are you going?", he asked.

'Boy don't question me! Why are you in my bed, and where are your pants? Mikasa was stunned to see her little cousin, all six foot two inches of him, in his boxers and socks, chilling like he was at home in his own bedroom. She wrapped her comforter around her body trying to shield herself from her cousins' gaze, and he had the audacity to look at her as if he belonged there and was doing nothing wrong. He advanced toward her with his arms outstretched.

"Mikasa, come on now it's just me Brandon; your favorite cousin."

'My favorite cousin? Why is my favorite cousin in my bedroom, in his drawers?

He moved closer completely ignoring what she said.

Don't come any closer, just answer!'

"I had to see you to apologize for what happened last night. It really wasn't intentional. I would never hurt you Mikasa, you know that. I didn't mean to touch you *there*; that was a mistake. I have been texting and calling all day to apologize. Why didn't you answer?"

I was pissed, and completely puzzled now. My 200-pound cousin was in my bedroom, in his underwear, halfheartedly apologizing for what occurred at *his* prom the night before by disrobing and lying up in my bed. Am I being punked? Is this for real?

'Why didn't I answer? Why didn't *I* answer?

Okay, so you came here, took off your clothes, got in my bed and were doing only God knows what to me, and now that you woke me up, you are sorry for touching me *there*!? And you touching me *there,* was feeling my butt Brandon, so what about the kiss? That preceded you feeling my butt. How are you going to apologize for that? Oh wait, I better not even ask that considering what you are doing here now. This is ridiculous, and none of it should have ever happened! We are cousins Brandon, why are you behaving like this? Why did you kiss me on the lips? Do we ever kiss each other on the lips, and more importantly, do you sleep in my bed *Brandonnnnn*?'

"We used to sleep together all of the time, or have you forgotten?"

'Are you serious, *Brandonnnn*? Have I forgotten what? When we were little, over ten years ago? I am sixteen now, and you are fourteen. You are too old, and too damn big to be sleeping in my bed!'

"Really, Mikasa? I was in your bed last week, so stop it. And stop dragging my name out like that; you only say it like that when you are angry."

'Well in case you have not noticed *Brandonnnn,* I am angry! Very angry! This is my personal space, and we are teenagers now not little kids. Last week we were in my bed watching movies, and that was the extent of it, and you know that I wasn't in bed when you woke up. In fact, I'm so good to you, such a nice cousin, Brandon, that I slept in my moms' room so that I didn't have to wake you, to move into your own bed. You do have one here, you know. You don't belong in mine.'

Mikasa, please, my bed, your bed, they are in the same house, so what does it matter? Just don't be mad about this. I did come here to apologize, and I hate it when you're mad at me. We have already spent half of our life on this very bed, so why are you tripping?"

'What do you mean, why am I tripping? This is my bed, in my room, and this is my body. I'm tripping because this here, what you did to me, is so inappropriate. You, being in my bed in your drawers rubbing up on me, that is *sooo* wrong. You kissing me, and feeling my butt last night at your prom, that was just dead wrong. When does it stop? I shouldn't have to tell you any of this Brandon. You know better! Just because we are close and have been for a long time, you have to remember that I'm your cousin. I did you a favor when I agreed to go to your prom with you because your girlfriend was sick, but now, you are adding insult to injury by climbing up in my bed, in your drawers and caressing me!
What is going on with you lately? We are first cousins. And let me break that down for you, just in case you don't understand what that means. Do not kiss me on the lips, don't touch my butt, don't get in my bed, don't…., oh just let's not touch each other at all anymore, okay? First cousins, hell, family just doesn't do that!'
Mikasa was pissed and leaving the room because it was apparent that Brandon was not moving. Brandon reached for her, and she flinched.

Now, Brandon was pissed too and putting on his clothes. He began to talk to himself.

"I don't believe her. Why is she so upset? We are so close and always have been. All the family envies our relationship. I have always been her favorite person, period. She barely sees or spends time with any of the family besides me. She does everything with me, and I spend every weekend here in this house. Aunt Patti adores me and considers me as her son. Why is she acting like I don't belong here with her?

# MIKASA
## BLURRED LINES: BOOK 1
# COCOA BROWN

PRETTY PURSE MEDIA

# Chapter One – HOW IT ALL BEGAN

I am Mikasa, a five-foot two brown skin beauty. I just turned sixteen a month ago and I am on my way to Vassar in August where I will double major in Economics and Japanese. My father, Darius Jones, isn't ready for me to go to college. He can't accept that I am growing up but despite that, I love my father and he has to know that it is time for him to let me grow not let me go. He is my first love, my protector, my rock. And how would I describe him? Well, he is the epitome of strength, love, and success. He is intelligent, handsome, and overprotective to a fault. No one compares to my father, except of course my mom. She is my heart, the one that I trust with everything, the one who soothes me and always pushes me to excel without fear or compromise. Yes, Mommy is first, but Dad is the closest second; they are the absolute best parents a girl could ever have.

What, you don't believe me? Well, all my friends and family say so and for that reason and quite a few others I will never understand, for the life of me why these two incredible people aren't together. I mean, parents are supposed to be together and these two, they never argue, well except when it comes to my cousin Brandon and that's a whole other story. Brandon, Aunt Sara's son, brings out the worst in my dad, but anyway, I digress. Now getting back to my two favorite people, I have to say that my parents are strange like that, because they are always all up in each other's business but still remain apart after eleven years. My mother, sweet Patti Jones, still wears her wedding ring and keeps my fathers' name, and I can't figure them out right now but eventually, I will find a way to get them back together. I am at that age now where their excuses for being apart just don't make sense anymore and haven't for some time now. I will be moving away to college soon, away from them both and it's time for them to kick loose and really enjoy their lives together, instead of pretending that there are real reasons for them to stay apart.

The background on them, you know, the real story is not that unique, just a bit disturbing and quite disappointing to my grandparents. Mom and Dad had me at a young age. Mom was only seventeen and in her sophomore year of college when she discovered that she was four months pregnant. When my mom finally told my grandparents, she refused to listen to reason and was adamant about marrying my dad before I arrived. Nana and Papa, my grandparents, continued to protest about the impending marriage, but with Mom's belly showing at that point, Nana finally acquiesced and accompanied them to the courthouse along with Darius' father to make it official. Despite their commitment to one another, and the love that they shared which was obvious to everyone who met them, my grandfather refused to attend the wedding. My Dads' mom had already passed years before meeting my mom. After the wedding and for many years after that, my grandparents were still disappointed. Anytime that they saw my father all that ran through my grandparent's minds was the thought that Patti planned to be the first doctor in the family and now she was pregnant at seventeen, like half of the other fast girls in the neighborhood. My grandparents wondered how this could have happened to their sweet Patti. They expected this type of behavior from their other daughter, my Aunt Sara. She was the rebellious one, the one always trying to get a rise out of her parents with her daily antics. Patti, on the other hand, had always been passive, sweet, and excelled in school. She made it to the honor roll all throughout school, always adhered to curfew, never talked back or voiced objections to the house rules or chores and lovingly adored her parents. She had such an easy-going, sweet personality and was the joy and delight of their lives. This is precisely why her pregnancy turned their lives upside down. It never should have happened that way and instinct told my grandfather to keep Darius away from his precious daughter, but the polite young man blindsided him by approaching her through schoolwork. Grandpa was so preoccupied with overtime at work that he missed all the signs that his daughter was slowly and steadily falling in love.

# DARIUS JONES: HIS SIDE OF THE STORY

My name is Darius and I just turned seventeen a few weeks ago. My life consists of basketball, academics, and my Pops. Life is pretty good for me besides missing my mom every day since she passed, but right now I have my eye on this beautiful girl that I have been watching for years. Whenever I see her in the park or at the corner store, I make it my business to speak to her and try to buy her something, anything to stall her for a moment so that we can talk, but of course she always politely refuses. One day I saw her walking by my fathers' liquor store, and I ran up on her so fast, which caught her off guard, said hello and grabbed all her books out of her hand before she could react. I said, 'You know, I really, really like you, Patti.'

I couldn't afford to be shy any longer, so I continued. 'We have been neighbors for years and I am having some difficulty with my schoolwork. Do you mind if I ask your dad if you could help me study?'

She gave me the once over and had me feeling so tense as she pondered over my question. So, I continued.

'I have heard that your father is strict, but I would really appreciate your help and I don't mind asking him.' Patti kept staring, so I kept on talking.

'I need an A in my Physics class, and I see that you have the same book for that course. Can you help me?'

I was anxious, but I finally paused to watch her consider my request. She looked as though she was forming her mouth to say no, but I didn't want to panic prematurely so I remained silent and patient.

"I don't know. How do you know my name, and about my father?"

'Your neighbor Omar is in my class. I heard him talking about you one day, and he said something about your father. Aren't you friends with him? Do you think he would mind me asking you to help me?'

"We speak, but we aren't close. And, as for me helping you, I have a heavy load of schoolwork myself and I can't afford to compromise my grades for, what's your name again?"

'My name is Darius.'

"I don't think I can do that for you Darius but my sister…

I interrupted, 'I have seen you in the library with your friends studying. I like the way you speak to them, the way you coach them through the lessons. Listen, I'm embarrassed enough asking you, please don't pawn me off on your sister. I don't know what I can do to persuade you; what type of things do you like? Music, movies, whatever you want in exchange for your help, I can get it for you. But please, not your sister.'

I had to smile at that. He acted like he knew my sister.

We continued to walk and talk, and she asked, "Don't they have tutors at your school that can help you? I don't even know you, and I would think that you would be more comfortable with someone from your own school. And did you say that you saw me in the library? When was that?"

'Come on, I go to your school Patti, and the library that I saw you in is there….

We were a block away from her house, so she reached for her books, but I insisted on carrying them to the door.

Patti thought about the days that she noticed him in the lunchroom or saw him on the basketball court shooting hoops. He was the only boy at the school that she found attractive, respectful, and mature enough to deal with, but she refused to be taken advantage of.

"I'll think about it Darius and thanks," she said as she gestured toward her books.

Fast forward to the courthouse and I can say now that I knew that she never stood a chance with my charm and good looks. And I know that I'm a catch, but I also know that what I found in her was something rare, pure, and beautiful, and I absolutely had to have her, and I wasn't backing down on that. Not at all.

The ceremony was short and sweet, nevertheless, Patti's father still refused to attend. After the ceremony I moved my beautiful wife into the home my father provided for us. It had been a rental property for years and was recently vacant of tenants. We renovated it together; my father and I, in preparation of this very moment.

I was nervous about starting a family, but it was also the happiest day of my life.

## PATTI JONES: HER SIDE OF THE STORY

So, I'm walking from school minding my own business, and this guy is in my face, and has my books out of my hands, and into his before I can protest. Allow me to introduce myself, my name is Patti, I'm an honor student, head of the Debate Club and head of the French Club. I enjoy school tremendously, and attend basketball games sometimes, between my club meetings, and I will be a doctor, so guess what? I don't have time to waste on boys but, there is always a but, I had to admit that I did recognize him and knew his name, when we finally came face to face, and Darius is fine, *but* I never let anything, or anyone, get in the way of my studies. So many guys were in my face, all the time, so what made him so different?

Well, I had to admit to myself, that I noticed him, and had seen him several times before he approached me, and I didn't know much about him besides that he was older, an athlete, and seemed to be a decent guy. So, initially when he approached me, I didn't think much of it. He asked if I could help him with his studies, and I was a bit surprised and figured that most athletes didn't have to ask for much of anything since everything was given to them all the time. So, when he asked, I listened, and wanted to say no, but he persisted. He offered me anything that I wanted, just to tutor him so reluctantly, and eventually, I said yes.

We began to meet daily and, I must admit, that like my father, Darius was kind and genuinely concerned about my well-being. I was there to assist him in excelling in Physics and thought that our sessions were supposed to be all about that with him, but every day, after I agreed to "tutor" him, he met me after school, with lunch in hand and insisted that we eat on the bench, outside of the library, before beginning our study sessions. Surprisingly, he always brought good stuff that I liked to eat, and he studied my face and my responses when we spoke, as if he never wanted to forget any of what I said or did. Every day that we met, which was every day except weekends he always inquired about the events that occurred the prior evening, my interactions with my family, how I slept, how my classes were, how other students got along with m, and if anything, or anyone was bothering me. Darius questioned me non-stop, from the moment I got out of school, up until the moment he dropped me off on my doorstep, and it was not long before he started inviting me to all of his games.

Before I knew it, we were studying every day and exclusively for weeks on end, and he never had a problem with any of the material that we covered. He asked a lot of questions, and often presented a fresh perspective that I had not considered. As time went on, I often wondered if he even needed a tutor because he was so bright and inquisitive. We studied and studied and studied and one day, when he got to my door, he kissed me, and I didn't resist him. The kiss was light and quick, but I liked it, and I looked at him with surprise on the outside but delight on the inside.

Fast forward to the present, here we are, at the courthouse trying to contain a love that is all consuming. It is heat in my bones and my belly every day. Who knew that someone I never even considered dating would become my husband and father of my only child? Who knew that all those years ago, and I cannot say exactly when, that he would steal my heart.

## CHAPTER TWO - 16 YEARS LATER

## MIKASA

I am at Presbyterian Hospital watching my mom complete her rounds in the pediatric ward and she is so calm and beautiful. I don't know how my dad does it. I mean, it has been eleven years! *How could he bear to be separated from her for eleven years?*

But anyway, he had been pretending to resist my mother for all these years, and it must be unbearable for him. Earlier today on the phone, this was the routine with my father.

'How is your mother? Is she dating? Has she been hanging out lately? How is work?'

As usual, I would reply, "Didn't you just see her last night, Daddy? "Then he would laugh and say, 'Tell your mother I said hello and that I love her.' "Okay, Daddy", was my standard reply. My dad was always at the house, and my mom always left little notes around the house, letting him know that she knew that he was snooping around her place. My mom had her purse now and was heading in my direction.

'Hey Baby-Girl, how are you today?' Her smile was electric. "Fine Mom, how are you?" We headed to her car to go on our bi-annual lingerie spree for pretty under things, then on to the Cheesecake Factory, in White Plains, NY. We got in her Mercedes CLK, which was her only indulgence as a professional woman, and drove off.

"Mom, I'm so excited and scared about college. I mean, I dread being away from you, but I am excited too! Would you believe that Aunt Sara and Daddy don't want me to go? They both want me to stay "local," like an hour away is so far. They act like I'm still a baby. Daddy doesn't think that I'm ready, but the school is so close, and I am sixteen not ten. What's wrong with them Mommy; or is it me?"

My mom chuckled and sighed. 'Mikasa, you know that it's not you. Your dad hates the fact that you have grown up so fast, and unlike most other teens your age, he is losing you a couple of years early. All your life, you have advanced so quickly before our eyes that sometimes we both feel a little left behind. And your Nana felt the same way about me. We can't help feeling so attached to our only child, and you know that Aunt Sara swears that you are her daughter too. So, I didn't expect anything less from her, and that's why she spoils you so much. And let's not talk about your father. He never, ever wants you to grow up but me, you know that I 'm always realistic about things so, I know that we really can't stop your progress. I just go with it even though I get choked up thinking about losing you so soon too.

When children go away to college, they begin their life apart from their parents and things just are never the same again. We all must come to grips with the fact that you have so much to do in this world, so much potential; you're growing up, moving quickly and will do more than any of us can even imagine. We can't stop that; we just have to roll with it.'

I looked at my mom. "You always know just what to say. You understand me and what I'm going through, and you never seem to let your feelings or desires interfere with any of it. You're simply incredible, and that's why I love you so much.

But honestly, as far as my potential goes; how much more can I do in this world Mom? I mean, you are a doctor, the best at the hospital, Head of Pediatrics. Daddy is a successful businessman and investor. I can only pray that I will be as prosperous, compassionate, and successful as you both are. I have some incredibly large shoes to fill."

Mom chuckled again and said, 'Contrary to what you believe, we expect a lot more from you baby girl, the bar is extremely high. And don't worry about your dad and aunt, they will come around, and if not, they will build a bridge and get over it. Vassar here we come!'

We both laughed as we pulled into the mall. After hours of searching through racks and piles of pretty panties and bras we exited victorious with several bags in each hand. We headed across the pavilion as Mom's phone began to ring. She shifted her bags to one hand, grabbed her phone from her purse, and answered the phone.

'Hello? Oh, hi Brandon, how are you? Yes, Mikasa is with me.' I gasped forgetting that I had to practice with Brandon this afternoon. Mom gave me a look. 'Hold on Brandon.' Mom passed me the phone.

"Brandon?"

Mikasa, what happened? You forgot all about me, didn't you?

"B, I apologize, let me get you something to eat to make up for it. What would you like from the Cheesecake Factory?" I knew that would soften him up quick.

'So, you think you can fix it by feeding me? Well…

Come on Brandon, I apologized. What would you like to eat?

He sighed long, but then he ordered two entrees, a salad and two pieces of cheesecake. "Dag boy, you are so greedy! I sure won't forget about you again." I laughed and told him goodbye and checked my wallet.

My mother said, 'You know that boys' prom is next week, and he acts like he still doesn't know how to dance. Are y'all making progress?'

"He is doing fine Mom. He acts like he has two left feet but every time that we practice, he out dances me. He wants to be perfect for his prom and for *Kim*. He even has the tango down pat, and by the way, who does the tango anymore? This dude is too fancy if I say so myself, but Kim is sure to be impressed.

As we finished our meal and I ordered Brandon's food Mom said, 'You know that boy is so spoiled! Who does he think is paying for all of that?'

I apologize Mom if I didn't forget about him, you wouldn't have to foot the bill. You know that he thinks that he's the son that you never had. He is worse than me.'

We laughed and ordered our dessert. I continued, "I am so glad that the prom is next week because that boy is monopolizing all my free time. When I leave school, he's there, when Jada and I hit the track to run he's there, when we go to Coldstone or the movies he is there too. He is everywhere, all the time and Jada loves it because she has a crush on him, but I need my space.

For years, Brandon has been bragging about being the best friend/cousin/brother I could ever have and believe me only you and Dad are closer to me, but I like to have time with my home girl alone. I need time to talk about girl stuff and check out the boys. No one, and I mean no one can get close to me with Brandon around. Guys always think that he's my man. He is always holding or touching my arm or shoulder and I'm tired of it.

After this dance he needs to ease up some and let me explore. Please talk to him Mommy. I tried to tell him before, but he always says I'm hurting his feelings, and he doesn't want to hear it. He says that I'm pushing him away like his mother does. I hate to hear that and see him sad, but he is working my nerves. Do you know that he was at the movies on Saturday when Jada and I went out? I swear if he doesn't eavesdrop on every call that I make and treating me like I'm the baby cousin! And whenever I discuss us hanging out with our own friends, he always throws you in the mix saying that you told him to look after me. The nerve! I don't understand when he makes time to practice and do his own thing.

Mommy looked at me and agreed. I know you girls do need time to hang out alone, but I didn't realize that it bothered you that much. What is really going on Mikasa?

What do you mean? Nothing is going on Mom, I mean, well I think that I like this boy. He lives around Jada's block. His name is ......

'Pooch,' my mother said.

I sat back surprised. "How could you know that, Mom? You are always working, and I don't remember you coming to Jada's lately. Who told you, Brandon? See what I mean?"

'Brandon didn't tell me anything. I heard you say his name on the phone last week. How old is he, Mikasa? Where does he go to school?'

"I don't know; Mom I guess he is about eighteen. Due to your nephew's interference, I have not been able to say more than hello to him. Jada thinks that he works at the gym on Fordham Road.

And he is fine."

Mom looked at me inquisitively and smiled.

'He's fine, is he? My little girl is growing up. You think that you like this boy, now do you? He must be something special because I don't remember you mentioning any other boy to me, ever. Just make sure that you take your time and get to know him before you get too excited about this boy.

I'm going to let you know now that we are alike in so many ways. We love deeply. So, make sure that you continue to talk to me like you are talking to me now because, sometimes, love can make you feel like nothing else matters and I don't want you to lose your focus. I value your honesty, and trust your choices, but keep in mind that there is more to a boy than his looks.

Also, remember that I am only half of the equation when it comes to things like this. If I know anything about your father, he knows more about this boy than you do. If you meet him and you like him, be patient with your father Mikasa, and trust him. If anything is questionable, or out of order about this boy, your father will detect it, and not allow him to come anywhere near you. Believe and understand that.

Now, as far as Brandon is concerned, I will talk to him and keep him busy this weekend, to give you a break from practicing with him. I understand how you feel about him being all up in your space, but it has been so comforting to know that for all these years he had your back, and you were safe. As an only child I worried about you being raised alone, then two years later came Brandon, and instantly it was like you had a baby brother. You two were like peas in a pod, and you know as well as I do that it will be hard on him when you move away to school, but we will get through it together. He has a little girlfriend now, and you may be dating soon so it should work out just fine.'

I reminisced for a moment about our shared childhood. We did have a lot of fun together; Brandon and I. Mom's voice, calling my name, shook me from my reverie. She left the tip, we grabbed our bags, and left the restaurant.

## DARIUS JONES – Raising Mikasa

It wasn't easy at first, adjusting to being home all day alone with our baby but I found my groove and really enjoyed raising Mikasa. The ducky baths, nursery rhymes, trips to the park, watching Barney and even changing pampers brought me joy. Mikasa had such a great disposition, she ate without a problem, and she had the most infectious smile and laugh that kept us going for hours on end. The other part that I loved about taking care of home was the look of excitement on my wife, Patti's face when she returned home each afternoon from school and the attention and intensity of emotion that Patti showered on me every evening after she laid Mikasa down to sleep for the night was simply incredible.

Her energy level continued to amaze but it was clear that nothing would derail her plans of becoming the first doctor in the family and I supported her every step of the way. I also was determined not to disappoint her parents by compromising their dream for her with my carelessness.

I didn't mean for things to happen quite the way they did. I wanted to marry Patti before we were intimate. I really wanted to wait because I had the plan for our life together all worked out in my head. But when Patti was in my arms kissing and touching me, my plan was the farthest thing from my mind. When we finally started dating after months of tutoring, I was pressed up on her whenever we managed to be alone. The pent-up emotions, the desires I fought to contain for months, were brimming over and pushing me to the edge every time that we spent time together, which seemed to be every day now including weekends.

But when Patti began to volunteer at the hospital during the summer, I felt lost. I was so accustomed to getting my Patti fix, every day for hours at a time that I didn't know how to behave at first, with so much free time on my hands. My father noticed the change in my behavior when Patti wasn't around and began to teach me everything that there was to know about his various businesses. He witnessed firsthand how intensely I loved Patti, and he constantly admonished me about being respectful with her and her body. He was a busy man, and most of the time that we spent together was at work, but he knew that the more time that I spent exclusively with Patti, increased our chance of being intimate and he was adamant about me being responsible for all my actions.

It was just him and I since I lost my mom at such an early age, and he did his best to teach me all that he knew about women. And he did that on a day-to-day basis by explaining to me exactly what I needed to accomplish to secure my relationship and plan a fulfilling life with Patti.

"You need goals son. I understand that you like to be around Patti every waking minute but as a man you have to learn be patient, use wisdom and stay focused on what is ahead of you, not just what's in front of you right now. You have to pace yourself, so that you are successful in planning for your future. We will work together to line things up so that you can run these businesses, maximize your own investments, and secure property for residual income. I know that Patti wants to be a doctor. I understand what she is focused on. What do you want to be son?"

'I am Patti's protector, her husband, her future, her everything.'

"Okay, that sounds good, but what are you going to do for you? You know that I haven't had your mom around for a while now, but my question to you is how are you going to remain interesting and relevant to Patti as the two of you grow together if she is your only interest?"

'Listen Dad, I don't need anything else. I love Patti and she loves me, what else matters?"

I would often say this to my father, to end the conversation, shrug off his advice and try to circumvent all that he fought to teach me. I only wanted to be with Patti, and I didn't want anyone else around her.

But my father was so patient with me, and he cautioned me about my feelings. He would admonish me about my emotions running too high and too hot for Patti. It took some time, but eventually, I learned to control them a bit.

"Darius, you need to understand that as your father I tell you things to help not hinder you. I want to see you grow into the best man that you can be, and to accomplish that you need interests of your own. Your mother and I had a great relationship because we took time to develop ourselves individually, which kept us excited about being together. I understand and know exactly how you are feeling right now because I felt the same way about your mother way back when, but I also knew that I had to hold her interest any way possible, and the easiest way to do that for me was to be successful at something that I loved doing.

You are very intelligent son, but I sense that you have no interest in college, and I don't have a problem with that, but you have to be good at something. These businesses are yours to run but you will learn all about them and respect all the effort that I put into them.

I know that you can take them all to another level, but the interest must be there, and it must be genuine. Just think about all that I'm telling you and be wise about your choices."

I looked at my dad, acknowledged what he said and headed towards the door to get my girl. Patti and I continued to meet every day when I picked her up from the hospital. She got so much attention from boys and men alike there and it increased when we began dating and that frustrated the heck out of me.

Not to be cocky, but it was amazing to see that the love that we shared gave her an untouchable glow that attracted people to her beauty and personality everywhere that we went. There was always some boy, man, or child in Patti's face when I arrived to pick her up, and it tried my patience as Patti kindly dealt with patients, visitors, and staff alike. She wasn't fazed or affected by the constant attention she received from other men and people in general. As I approached her and stopped to let her finish her sentence and acknowledge me, my mood stabilized. It was Friday and I was anxious to grab Patti and leave. I saw the look in the doctor's eyes as he spoke to her, and I watched his gestures. When he finished speaking, Patti turned around and said, 'Hi babe, how are you?' My heart softened and I relaxed as the doctor turned to leave.

"Hello Patti. I'm fine now that I see you. Are you ready?" Patti removed her jacket, grabbed her bag, and headed for the door.

"You look so good, as usual. How are you, how was your day?"

'It was fine, but my head is hurting a little. Can we stop by your house for a bit? I just want to lie down for an hour before we do anything tonight.'

I was taken aback. I had been dying to get Patti to the house for so long and now that she asked, I paused.

'You know that if I go home, my dad will want me to stay in for the night. I just want to lie down for an hour, and I should be fine.'

Sure, Patti. In my head I knew that my dad expected to be around when I had female company, but what came out was, "Of course you can rest at my house. My room is all yours Patti.'

I said this with my mouth, but I could already feel the excitement surging all through my body. Patti smiled as I held her hand and walked her to the car. I don't remember driving home, parking or walking inside of my house. What I do remember though, is feeling Patti's body against mine, on my bed, and that night was our downfall. Or should I say, my downfall. Where was my self-control? Well, fast forward, and here we are now, in love, and married with a child.

## BRANDON

I was watching television when I finally heard the keys in the door. Aunt Patti and Mikasa came through the door, loaded down with bags. My eyes caught the pink bags, and instantly, I wondered what was in Mikasa's. I got up, scooped the food bag out of her hand, and walked away. Mikasa groaned, and I turned around grabbing all the bags out of her hand and turned to my aunt and grabbed hers. I went to my aunts' room first to drop her bags down and then I took my time with Mikasa's' bags peeking in to see all her lace goodies. I thought to myself, I can't wait to see her in these. Then I frowned and quickly returned to my food.

Mikasa came over to me and apologized again for forgetting to meet me as she ran her hand over my head. I loved her touch and felt guilty about having that feeling. I waved her off so that I could enjoy my food and to make her think that I didn't like the attention, but I loved it when she touched me. She popped me in the back of my head and smirked at me. Of course, she looked as good as ever in her shorts and halter top. I couldn't help but admire my gorgeous little cousin.

We had been practicing dance for weeks for my school prom and I didn't tell her yet that she would be my date. I was dating this girl Kim from my school, and I asked her to go to the prom, but I planned to fake her out with some illness on the day of the prom. She was a thirsty chick clamoring to be with a baller, so I felt little remorse about blowing her off for prom. I thought that if I tried dating a beautiful girl it would take my mind off my cousin, but it seemed as if girls only saw dollar signs whenever I appeared in their line of vision. I hated that. They also couldn't wait to sex me, and they all knew that I was only fourteen because I was always honest and told them. Fast girls: and they all seemed so easy except for Mikasa. She is the only virgin that I know. Even Mikasa's' best friend acts as if I can get it and I barely pay her any mind at all.

'Brandon, Brandon? Don't you hear me talking to you? I called your mom to let her know that you are staying over tonight to practice.'

Sorry Auntie. I was daydreaming and enjoying my food. I figured that you would say that anyway so I brought clothes with me so that I can go straight to school in the morning. And I think that I still have clothes back in the room anyway, so I'm good. Oh, and thank you for dinner. You're so good to me Auntie and you're letting me stay tonight, I love you so much!

'You're welcome, Brandon. How is basketball practice coming along? I haven't heard from your coach lately. Are you doing everything that you're supposed to be doing?' Brandon sighed. Aunt Patti, you know that I'm the MVP. You won't hear any complaints from Coach Ted about me. I'm still his favorite, and you have not heard from him because I asked him to stop calling you. He is just trying to mack anyway, and I'm not having it. I don't appreciate any man trying to push up on you!'

I couldn't believe this boy. He is only fourteen and he's acting like he runs things, but I couldn't help but laugh at him.

'You're a mess boy! That man is not thinking about me. When he did call, it was only to discuss your performance and your academics, nothing else. Brandon gave me the side eye like please Auntie.

I ignored him and said, "By the way, I need your help this weekend. There are some things that I want to pick up to spruce this place up a bit. I need to get supplies from Home Depot.'

Is Mikasa going? I asked casually.

"No baby, she's hanging with Jada this weekend.'

I sighed, all right Auntie, whatever you need.

I ignored the sound effects he made and said, "Good, I haven't spent much time with you lately. We need to talk and catch up.'

She hugged me and went to her room to change. I got up and threw away all the food containers and washed my hands. After I dried them thoroughly, I went into the living room to practice with Mikasa. She was in her pajamas freshly showered with her hair pinned up. Mikasa put in the CD, but I said, 'I have the fast songs down already. Put on Dru Hill so that we can try slow dancing again.

We both assumed the position, my hand on the small of her back, her hand in mine with her other hand on my shoulder. She had her slippers on, so she barely reached my chest, and I was towering over her.

Mikasa please put on your heels like always. You know that my date will have on heels. I liked the feel of Mikasa's' cheek resting on my chest while we danced. She grabbed her heels which boosted her up a few inches. Her father hated her in heels, but I loved it because it brought her that much closer to my face. I held her in the proper position careful not to touch any part of her that I wasn't supposed to, but as "Beauty" played I unconsciously pulled her closer to me.

Mikasa was drowsy as she went through the motions, and she was moving slowly as she laid her head on my chest. Aunt Patti came out refreshed from her shower,, and caught a glimpse of me holding Mikasa close, and singing softly in her ear with my eyes closed.

"I'm hoping I can make you mine before another man steals your heart" … Beauty was my favorite song.

Aunt Patti cleared her throat, and when I opened my eyes, I could see that she was not pleased.

'Are you two sleep-dancing?'

She didn't wait for a reply, she turned off the music and said, 'Let Mikasa rest.'

Aunt Patti's voice roused Mikasa, and she stepped back from me. I was disappointed because we didn't even get through one song, but I didn't show it. I scooped her up off the floor, and in my arms carried her to her room. I placed her gently on her bed and slipped off her shoes. I covered her with the sheet and sat on her chaise watching her. Aunt Patti waited for me to return to the living room and when I didn't, she came to the room and found me sitting in Mikasa's room in a chair by her bed, watching her sleep.

My aunt spoke softly so as not to disturb Mikasa. 'Come on son, go to bed.' Reluctantly I got up and headed toward the bathroom. A few moments after that, my head was under the shower and so many emotions ran through me. I just couldn't understand what I was feeling and thinking about my own cousin.

Why did I feel this way about her and exactly why was it wrong to love her like this? I mean I don't, can't think about any other girl the way I think of Mikasa. It is so confusing and frustrating because, I feel like I always have to touch her, and it seems as if she is sensing it and pulling away from me more lately because of it. Well, she doesn't know it, but boy do I have a surprise for her.

## MIKASA

I don't even remember getting in my bed last night, but here I am getting ready, and off to school I go, after having breakfast with Mom and Brandon. He's acting spacey and looking at me with googly eyes and Mom seemed so distracted.

I kissed them both on the forehead and went out the door to school. I couldn't wait to tell Jada that we would be hanging out together this weekend thanks to my Momma and thank God it is Friday.

So, who is Jada? She is my best friend, who just turned eighteen and happens to be the coolest girl in our entire senior class. We have practically every class together, which is only three on Fridays. I usually go to the library after that and then to Brandon's basketball practice on Fridays but today we were heading straight to her block; Fordham Hill and guess who was standing outside when we arrived? Pooch.

As soon as we got off the bus, he walked over to meet us. He motioned for me, and I nodded at him. Now that I finally got to meet him, I decided to play with him a little. I kept heading towards Jada's building with her and he called my name.

'Mikasa.'

I turned slightly and he said my name again softly. I stood there.

'Mikasa, hold up; come and talk to me for a minute. Do I have to chase you?'

Yes, you do, I replied. It made him pause for a minute and smirk at me.

'I'm asking you nicely, come and talk to me.' He walked towards me.

Jada and I stood still to let him catch up and he glanced at Jada.

"What are you two getting into tonight? Jada, can I talk to your girl for just a minute? My cousin is in front of your building, and I know that he wants to see you."

Jada glanced at me, and I said, 'Let me go and check in with her mom. We will be back.'

"Alright, I will be out here and I'm glad that you shook your shadow. I thought I would never catch you alone."

I laughed and thought briefly about Brandon blocking any and every man from me. I turned to walk away, and Pooch touched my hand. When you come back down let's go eat somewhere okay?"

I paused, feeling sparks shoot up my arm from his touch.

I don't even know you, but we'll see, I said.

Jada and I walked towards the building in silence. When we got close, we could see Shane posted up on the wall waiting and Jada went up to him and kissed him. She let him know that we would be right back, he greeted me and said, 'Did she see my cousin?'

Jada nodded and we went upstairs. After sitting and talking with Jada's parents for an hour or so we freshened up and went back outside.

Before we saw Pooch and his cousin, Jada said, 'you know Pooch has been asking about you every day this week. He asked for your number, but I told him to get it from you. He told me that he wants to take you out, but I told him that he had to ask you himself. He has a car so we could go to City Island or One Fish, Two Fish tonight, it's your choice. So, what's up, what do you want to do?'

You know he is cute and all but, I don't know him like that, so I'm not getting in his car.

"Mikasa, you must be kidding? I know them both; I have known them for years. Are you that scared of your Daddy?"

'Listen girl; don't put my daddy in this. This is the first time that he is talking to me face to face for real, so I'm not getting in his car. What if he takes us somewhere that we don't want to go? What are you going to do?'

Jada looked at me and rolled her eyes. 'You get on my last nerve but okay. What about Jimmy's, we can walk there?' We both smiled at our decision made without them as we saw them approaching us.

They stopped a few feet from us, and Pooch just stared at me like he didn't just see me an hour ago. Shane and Jada started talking and laughing but we just stood still, watching each other.

## POOCH DAVIS

*I like her.*

I can't say exactly what it is, but there is something about her. I mean, it could be the pretty toes, her hair, her brown skin, those lips, man, so many reasons. She is so feminine; she moves like a lady; she speaks softly and smiles often, and her smile is so pretty.

I like her.

I've been coming through here for a minute and I haven't seen anyone quite like her. There are some pretty girls on Fordham Road and in the Bronx but this girl…

My cousin walked up to me closing the distance between us and said, 'how about we get something to eat?'

That sounds good. I continued to stare at Mikasa, and I said, 'I asked her before they went upstairs so let's see what they say. I have a feeling that we won't be driving anywhere, but if we do, here are the keys so you can drive.'

We walked up to meet them and Mikasa checked her phone, put it in her bag and glossed her lips.

She said hello to me like she didn't just see me an hour ago. I paused and felt something shift in my heart.

She spoke again and said, 'Are you ready to eat; how about some Hennessy Wings?'

I caught her glancing at my arms a few times and was glad that I wore a tank top.

Hennessy Wings sounds good, but I guess that means that you don't trust me enough to go farther than down the block with me. I don't bite Mikasa.

'Whether you bite or not is irrelevant. You don't know me, so why would you trust me in your car?' I smiled.

I liked her spunk. Okay so let's go to Jimmy's, my treat. We walked to the restaurant with the girls a few paces ahead of us. They stopped in front of the restaurant, and we caught up and opened the door for them to enter. The host approached and said,

'Table for four?' I came up behind Mikasa, lightly touched her arm and replied, 'two tables for two.' Mikasa looked at me as I motioned for her to follow the server to a booth deep in the back of the restaurant. It was a quiet corner and as Mikasa sat I slid in the booth beside her.

She seemed a bit startled and said, 'Why don't you sit across from me so that I can see your face while we eat? You have such a handsome face Pooch, how 'bout it?'

I paused for a moment, realizing that she was trying to work me already.

'Thank you for the compliment, but I would rather sit beside you if you don't mind. How about I turn my body to the side like this so that you can see my beautiful brown eyes when we speak?"

Mikasa smiled at me, but I could tell that she was accustomed to having her way, even without her saying a word.

The waiter approached, introduced himself and told us the specials. And even though we were side by side, his focus was clearly on Mikasa. He said, 'And what would the lady like to order?'

Mikasa smiled and said, 'We will have two virgin Strawberry Margaritas, a full order of Hennessy Wings, a Chicken Caesar salad, Sirloin Steak medium well with a loaded baked potato and sautéed onions and peppers on the side for the steak.' I looked at Mikasa then at the waiter and nodded. But I did not understand what just happened.

"What was that Mikasa?"

'What was what? Aren't you hungry? Did you want two steaks?'

"Huh?"

'Well, my mother always orders for my dad when we eat out and he loves it. What is the matter? Did I order too much? I do have money.'

I closed my eyes for a moment before I spoke. "You can order anything that you want but you need to know me and know exactly what I like before you can order for me. I'm not your Daddy *yet* so take your time. And I'm not like the boys that you are accustomed to dealing with either. I can walk, talk, and order my own food; I am a man."

'Okay so, yes, you are a man.'

Wow, she's challenging me already and it is just about lunch.

"Isn't that why you're attracted to me Mikasa? I'm not one of the schoolboys in your Science or Math class following behind you everywhere, doing whatever you say...

'Uh, where did that come from? I can see that you're a man Pooch, and in fact, the schoolboys who follow me around everywhere don't get upset as easily as you do.'

She said it, and smirked at me as if I was being ridiculous, but I continued.

"Okay, that's fair but tell me something Mikasa, are you even interested in getting to know me or am I just one on a list?'

Before she could answer the waiter returned with the drinks and sat them on the table. We thanked him and I waited for Mikasa to respond.

She took a sip of her drink and said, 'You know, that was a mouthful and I like you already! I like that you don't hold anything back. You say exactly what's on your mind. But who said that I was attracted to you? Jada? And what list are you referring to? The "I think you're different so I will give you special treatment like my dad gets list?'

I looked at her and instantly liked her even more because it was rare for me to be challenged by any woman.

'Don't you like steak Pooch?'

"Yes, I do."

'Do you like baked potato with everything?'

"Yes, I do."

'How about Margaritas and Hennessy Wings?'

"I do, but I wear the pants here, I am the shot caller. I make it happen. I said it and smiled, being sarcastic.

'Well forgive me for giving you special treatment. I eat out all the time so I thought that it would be cool to order for you, but I apologize for choosing things that you like without asking you but no harm, no foul right? It was meant to be a nice gesture, something to show you that yes, I am interested in you. I know that you aren't my Daddy. My Daddy is my first love, my first date and the best example I could ever have of what a good man looks like. He is the only man I can compare you to, and since you are talking about how things should be done, that's what I did with you.

All right, how about this since I seemed to have rubbed you the wrong way already why don't you tell me something. Just talk to me, tell me something no one else knows about you. Tell me about your family, the things that you like to do, where you go to relax, what upsets you, uh scratch that, I already have an idea of that, who your favorite person is and who means the most to you. Tell me who you are inside, what your purpose is; tell me your plans. Also, tell me what you want from me. Tell me, talk to me. I'm really interested.'

Damn, I thought to myself what have I gotten myself into? She's going to keep me on my toes and challenge me every step of the way. I looked at her staring deep into her eyes and then the food came.

We thanked the waiter as he sat all the dishes on the table, and we sat motionless for a moment. Mikasa held her gaze on me. She grabbed my hand and blessed and thanked God for the food. She took a wing and began to eat, still watching me.

"How old are you Mikasa?"

'How old am I? How old are you and don't try to turn the tables on me with that generic question. Answer the questions that I asked you then I will answer your question.'

She continued to eat the wings.

"I will Mikasa, but you didn't answer my other question. Am I on a list?

'A list for what? I said that I was interested in you and that I never dated anyone. If you're asking if there is a list of boys that like me, I would say yes but Jada would have to confirm that for you, and I'm not seeing anyone if that's what you mean.'

"All right so here is my story." I sighed deeply. "Nobody knows that I really miss my parents. I don't talk about it at all, but they died in a car crash over a year ago right before the first time that I saw you." I sighed again, not wanting to delve deeper into that. "I like to stay fit; eat right and work out. To relax I get weekly massages, deep tissue, full body massages and my favorite vacation destination so far is Hawaii. What angers me besides losing my parents is not finding the right words to express myself sometimes. My favorite thing in the world right now is being here with you. I'm a year away from obtaining a B.S. in Psychology from Hunter College. And my favorite person since the moment I saw you last year is you and I can't say why." I smiled.

Mikasa sat back taking in all that I said. We ate silently watching each other. In my head I was thinking I can't believe that I told her all of that. She got me open already and I haven't even kissed her.

Mikasa pushed her plate away with most of the food still on it. I ate everything on my plate and reached for her wings. She touched my hand and asked me to continue. I figured that I would toy with her for a bit, so I didn't answer and grabbed her salad too and continued to eat. She smirked and reached in her purse for her phone to check it. I continued.

"Okay so as far as my purpose is concerned, I volunteer with the Boys Club mentoring a few young boys. We play ball, go to the movies, I check in with their teachers about their academic progress and sometimes I just hang out with them to talk or help them with homework. I do the things with them that I would do anyway if I had a younger brother.

Now what I want from you; let me think about that and get back to you or what I would like to happen between us is a better question. I like you; I am interested in seeing you again and I am nineteen.

How about you?"

Mikasa sighed remembering his question. 'Well now that I know your age, I am reluctant to tell you mine. But I'm sixteen. I just turned sixteen.'

I sat back conflicted. And then I laughed a bit. Stop playing Mikasa, you and Jada graduate this year, don't you?

At that moment Jada and Shane walked over to our table. They slid into the other side of the booth.

Shane exclaimed, "'I'm stuffed. Y'all want to see a movie?'"

Mikasa said, 'I'm ready if you are.' I just wanted to get away from him and my answer. But first I needed to go to the restroom. Immediately.

She grabbed Jada's hand and they proceeded to the front of the restaurant. As soon as they entered the restroom Jada sensed that Mikasa's nervousness wasn't good.

""'What happened Mikasa?'""

'You didn't tell me that he was nineteen, Jada?'

'I didn't know that he was nineteen. What's the problem? Shane is nineteen, I am eighteen, you're eighteen right, or is your birthday later this year?'

No Jada, you know that I just turned sixteen.

""'Mikasa we're in the same class, so I forgot. So, what's the problem?'""

The problem is, well…., you see how he just paused when Shane suggested the movie. He's not trying to mess with a sixteen-year-old. I can tell. I can just tell.'

""'Please Mikasa relax. Do you know how long that boy has been watching and asking about you, and asking for your number? It must be over a year now, so I doubt if those two numbers are going to stop him from pursuing you.'""

Yeah, well that sounds good, but I feel like I am jailbait to him now and what about my father?

""'What about your father Mikasa, my goodness? Can we do anything at all without your father coming up? I mean, we are headed off to college soon. Is your father going with you?""

'Jada, you just don't understand. My father, my parents, they aren't having it. I just don't know. Well, actually, it doesn't matter anymore because this boy is not messing with me now.

""Oh, please Mikasa, you're so dramatic! We will talk about this later but right now, let's go see our men.""

I washed my hands, put a cherry jolly rancher in my mouth, put my lip gloss on and headed out behind her with a smile on my face even though my emotions were all over the place.

They came back to the table, and I looked over at them, and then at Mikasa and said, "You two go ahead, I'm taking her to the park up the block."

And just like that they left, and I paid the bill. I took Mikasa's hand, and we headed for the door. I leaned in to kiss her, paused, caught myself, backed up and then we walked up the block in silence.

Mikasa said, 'I could go upstairs to Jada's now if you are uncomfortable with me. I didn't think that you were that old and to answer the question you asked before, Jada and I are graduating in a few months, and I will be going to Vassar to begin double major studies. I should have already advanced several grades in school, and I could have started college at thirteen, but my parents wanted me to experience high school. I don't expect you to...

I couldn't resist any longer. I touched her face and kissed her softly at first then I held her there kissing her for what seemed like an hour; forgetting that we were outside, forgetting her age and everything that she just said. After a few moments she stopped me and smiled.

She started to speak again as we walked and I said, "Did that kiss back there feel like I am uncomfortable with you, and do you think that I want to part from you after only a little over two hours? It has been a year since I first saw you and I never thought that it would take so long just to speak to you, but I couldn't stop thinking about you and asking about you. But I never imagined you being only sixteen. Why did you have to be sixteen!

And your college, where is Vassar, upstate somewhere? Dag, am I too old for you? I just turned nineteen last month."

I stopped talking because I felt as if I was rambling.

We walked to the bench and sat down and Mikasa was deep in thought. She sighed and said, 'I don't have a problem with your age, but I just know that my dad will, and Vassar is in Poughkeepsie. It's about an hour from here, not that far.'

We were sitting there together, and I knew that she was saying something, but I was so focused on her lips, that I leaned toward her eager to kiss her again but from a distance a deep rumbling low voice barked, "Mikasa!"

She froze in place, and I sat back a bit gazing down the block trying to determine who was calling her name. A man that looked to be in his late twenties approached rapidly and as Mikasa turned to look in his direction, she gasped and said, 'Daddy.'

"Daddy?!" I smirked at her. Dude looked too young to be her father.

'I have to go Pooch!'

I stood up to keep her with me, but she rushed away and grabbed her fathers' hand trying to walk him in the opposite direction, away from me. I thought to myself, I knew she had to have a man. I'd seen him before but couldn't quite place the face, then it came to me and I mumbled to myself, 'Darius?'

He didn't hear me because Mikasa was drag/pushing him up the block.

'Daddy please stop and let's talk about this at home! Please, you are embarrassing me!'

I began to follow them until Mikasa turned towards me and said please, let me talk to my father first. She looked terrified so I stood there even though I felt that I shouldn't. The man looked upset as if he caught his girl cheating.

"Talk to me about what Mikasa? You will not see him anymore, ever. He is not for you.

He thought to himself that it could not be his daughter in front of Jimmy's Restaurant kissing somebody and out here in the park too. And unfortunately, after making the U-turn to come back and upon closer investigation he found that indeed, here she was.

He got really close to her ear and said, "I told you repeatedly Mikasa about public displays of affection and you don't even know that man!

I saw the way that the man held her arm and whispered in her ear and was disappointed.

Mikasa tried to explain but he cut her off. "Mikasa matter of fact, stop pulling my arm, take my keys and go sit in the car. I need to speak to him. You're trying to pull me away from him, but I'm not having it. Let me let him know right now that he will not see you again, ever. Then I will deal with you.

She was nervous and upset but she continued to plead.

'Daddy, please you are embarrassing me, I just….

I cut her off.

"I'm embarrassing you!? You are my daughter, and you're out here on the street letting a man you just met practically make love to you on a bench and you have the nerve to say that I'm embarrassing you?"

Mikasa looked at me from a distance, then back at her father and suddenly tears began to fall as she walked to her Dad's Benz. Mikasa's father sighed, looked at me long and hard then walked around and got in his car.

## MIKASA

I was crying and glaring at my father as he got in, took his keys, and started the car. We drove in silence as we passed Pooch, and I was so heated, hurt, and nervous that I could scream. At the end of the next block my father parked the car and turned it off. We sat quietly for about five minutes, and he handed me a tissue when I finally stopped crying. I felt defensive so I broke the silence.

'Daddy, listen, I know where this is going to lead and before you light into me about this, Mommy was supposed to tell you about me staying with Jada this weekend.'

He looked at me like I was out of my mind.

"What are you talking about Mikasa? I really don't like to see you cry and it's never my intention to cause that reaction in you. But this is the first thing you have to say to justify your actions? Do you want to put the blame on your mother, my wife? Are you trying to put your mother between us?

What I saw out there had nothing to do with your mother, or you staying out with Jada! You are sixteen years old now and you have a phone. You could have called me yourself! And are you saying that your mother gave you permission to stand out on the street and kiss a boy? Should I call and ask her that?

You and I have an agreement and we went over it many times. I schooled you on how boys should talk to and treat you. There is no touching or kissing in the street, and I also asked you to let me meet them first before you went with them anywhere. I had that discussion with you Mikasa. It was all about you and me, not your mother!

I am so disappointed in you right now that I can't see straight. And who is he anyway?"

'His name is Pooch. He….

"Who!? Is Pooch his real name? What's his last name? Where does he live? Where does he go to school? How old is he?

Answer me right now. Do you know him Mikasa? You had your lips on his. Do you know him?!"

I was silent and wanted to cry again but I didn't. Pooch and I probably spent the last three hours together, but I honestly could only answer one of the many questions my father posed to me.

"Do you understand how much your mother and I have deposited into you? And me teaching you by example exactly how a man should treat you? After all the dates that I have taken you on since you were five years old preparing you for what to expect and tolerate from a man and at the first opportunity that you get, you are out her on Fordham Road letting old boy take advantage of you on a park bench! Why Mikasa? I taught you better than....

I couldn't control it now; my sniffling interrupted him. Tears were streaming down my face again; I was really crying, and I couldn't stop the tears if I wanted to. I knew that my dad always hated to see me cry but he still had that stern look on his face that meant that he was not backing down.

Through sobs I said, 'Listen Daddy I know that we had an agreement and I know you've done a lot to raise me right. I didn't plan to kiss him outside on the street or anywhere else for that matter. I apologize for that. I did know or figure that I would see him today and I didn't expect to feel like this. You are asking me all these questions about him, and I don't know the answers, but we did talk in the restaurant about his character, his feelings, and his purpose. I didn't expect him to hold my interest like he did or else I would have called you so you could meet him. I didn't think he was about much. Honestly, I just liked the way that he looked, and I thought that we would just talk, and I would move on. But when he touched my face...

My father shifted in his seat like he didn't want to hear another word.

I could have stopped him from kissing me, I mean he didn't force himself on me and he wasn't taking advantage of me. I just felt something for him that I never felt for any other boy. I let him kiss me and I wanted him to kiss...

Dad interrupted.

"Alright Mikasa, just stop please."

My father had to steer the conversation away from my feelings. Even though I'm sixteen and graduating from high school, he didn't want to accept that I'm growing up and feeling like a woman.

I sat there looking at my father knowing that he hated that I was growing up and away from him right in front of his eyes.

"You're not thinking straight right now and that bothers me. You say that you like him but how much do you know about him Mikasa? How can you like what you don't know?"

I know how I feel Daddy. Of all the immature boys in my school and the ones on the street, I've never entertained them or let any of them concern me. But Pooch, I can't explain it, it's a feeling that I have, a comfort level we seem to have with each other. We were just getting to know one another this afternoon in the restaurant. We never had the opportunity before for over a year because Brandon was always around. I had my personal space today and he and I had a chance to talk and…please give me a chance with him Daddy and I will have all the answers for you and then some. We had an honest conversation; I like him, and he is nice.

'Give you a chance? I love you Mikasa. You are my daughter. You know, usually I am so calm and levelheaded with you. I don't like to raise my voice at you because you are my baby girl and I love you more than anybody in this world, but I'm not happy about this Mikasa. Not one bit. How did you expect me to react to seeing my child being kissed in the street by a man that I don't even know? Didn't I ask you to talk to me about any boy that you were interested in first? You knew that you would see him, but you didn't, couldn't even call me and let me know that you were spending the night at Jada's? You have two parents and we; you and I talk about everything Mikasa and you told your mother about this boy, but you couldn't take the time to fill me in? I had to catch you out here to find out that you weren't where I thought that you would be.

Are you and your mother hiding things from me now? I'm so angry at you, and I really don't want to be."

I bristled at the accusations. I didn't want my parents to argue about this.

My father started the car and before I knew it, he pulled up in front of the house and said, "Let's go inside. I need to know exactly what your mother knows about all of this."

# CHAPTER THREE –PATTI'S HOME

It was about 10:00pm and Mikasa was away for the weekend. I just enjoyed a luxuriating whirlpool soak, oiled my body, and slipped into my favorite silk short nighty. I was about to put one of my old movies on when the door slammed, and I heard voices. I slipped on my matching peach silk robe and tied it tightly about my waist.

Darius called out, 'Patti? Patti, are you up?' Without thinking about it I let my hair down and walked into the living room. Darius was pacing a bit with Mikasa behind him.

"What happened Mikasa?"

Darius turned to face me and caught his breath as he took me all in briefly. He loved me in peach-colored clothes and his eyes softened for a moment.

Mikasa began to speak, and he interrupted and said, 'Your daughter was on Fordham Road kissing a man. Did you know that she was with him or going to see him? Did you give her permission to date someone without talking to me, Patti? She said that they just came from a restaurant before he started making love to her on the street.'

I glanced at Mikasa; she looked sad and guilty. I exhaled and moved towards my *husband* to take his jacket off. He acted like he didn't want to be touched but he let me take it from him and hang it up in the closet.

"Can we sit and talk about this Darius? Let me get you something to drink." He gave me a look that said you are in just as much trouble as she is and then he spoke.

'I don't want anything to drink Patti, just answer my question.'

Mikasa rested her Louis bag on the side table and sat on the couch. "Okay, I will tell you whatever you want to know but can we sit and talk about this together?"

Darius continued to pace so I touched his arm gently and asked him to sit again. He sat on the love seat, and I sat close beside him. I did my best to diffuse the situation before turning to address our only child.

"Who were you kissing and why were you kissing him outside on the street Mikasa?"

"'I was kissing Pooch. I did not mean to kiss him outside. We went out to eat and ….

I interrupted.

"Where was Jada?"

"'With Pooch's cousin; we all went to the restaurant together and then they went to the movies. We just wanted to talk so we were sitting outside of the building in the park.'"

"So where is Pooch now?"

"Daddy snatched me up and left him in the park by Jada's building."

 Now it was Darius' turn to interrupt as he moved Patti's hand from stroking his knee in the soothing motion that he recognized as her attempt to calm him like she always did. He also noticed her lack of surprise or shock at the mention of the boy's name and her smooth line of questioning.

'Patti, do you know this man that *our* daughter is seeing? Do you two know something that I don't?'

"I never met him, but Mikasa did mention him to me a few days ago."

'A few days ago. Really? And neither of you could let me know about him?'

We looked at each other but didn't speak.

'Imagine my surprise as I was coming off the Major Deegan to see my daughter lip locked with some man on the street and you're just as calm and serene about it as a slow breeze on the beach because you knew about him already. Wow.

So, tell me, what exactly is going on here Patti, matter of fact, good night Mikasa. You go to bed and let me speak to your mother alone and we will get back to you about this in the morning young lady.'

I wanted to protest and discuss it as a family, but I knew that I was in for it now since he was sending our daughter out of the room. I was used to Brandon putting me in a precarious position with Darius but now it was Mikasa's turn.

As angry and confused as she was, Mikasa kissed us both and went to her room. As soon as her door closed, I spoke.

"You're upset and I understand but you act like the girl killed somebody. She is sixteen Darius not six and this is the first boy she has shown interest in and I know that I should've mentioned it to you when she told me, but I wanted to give her the opportunity to talk to the boy without interference from Brandon and I didn't think it was that serious. I didn't know that there would be a kiss. She made a mistake. I apologize to you baby, and her and I both acknowledge that we should've told you that she would be at Jada's' for the weekend but please cut her some slack. How many times has Mikasa disappointed you in sixteen years?"

'That is not the point Patti I ….

"How many? How many mistakes has she made and how many have we made? Mikasa has done nothing but make you proud over all these years. She always listens to us, and she adores you so when she slips up and makes a mistake you treat her like this?

I can tell that she was crying. Remember what we did seventeen years ago? Or are you so grown now that you've forgotten? Let's try to be reasonable here…

He interrupted.

'Reasonable?

This was not even her first date; I'm her father and you left me out of the loop.

Reasonable?

I didn't touch you for six months in the beginning of our relationship, but this boy gets to kiss my daughter the first day that he speaks to her. How do you figure that?'

I frowned wishing that I could take back that word.

'Do you know what's reasonable? Reasonable is letting me, the father, know what is going on in our daughters' life. Reasonable is letting me meet and grill the boy before he sees her. Reasonable is my wife not encouraging our daughter to date a man who is practically my age, he is a man, Patti. Reasonable......

I touched his thigh to convey my understanding, but he moved my hand off and continued.

Reasonable is letting me back in your life and forgiving me for a mistake that I made fourteen years ago. Reasonable... I could go on and, on all night, but you two don't listen to me or care for my input anyway, so what is the point?

Reasonable? You want me to be reasonable when you're not? That's not fair Patti.'

Mikasa stood right by her door listening to the conversation from the hall.

"Darius, I apologize. It was a last-minute decision that I made to let her hang out with Jada. I exercised poor judgment this one time and you are acting as if I leave you out of the loop with everything where Mikasa is concerned. You are over here all the time; you're at her school all the time. You have her schedule and mine. Whenever you call, I answer the phone or get back to you if I'm making my rounds. We've been separated for eleven years now, and you still have my key and come and go through here as you please. Both of our bedroom doors are open, and I know that you examine our rooms when you feel like it. We have no secrets from you, and I don't complain about any of it.

We both made mistakes here, Mikasa and I. But I'm not going to let you make this about us not being together Darius. That is another issue for another day and time. Just forgive us both for what happened today and let's discuss a solution.

'Well, isn't that the neat and tidy Patti way. Just move on, forgive, and discuss a solution. It's never about my feelings with you now is it, Patti!

I swear that I've never loved anyone as much as I love you, but you really drive me up a wall when it comes to us!

I'm upset and I really don't appreciate any of this. You want me to forgive and move on, but have you?

You're so selfish Patti! Our separation or even a discussion about it is always an issue for another day and another time when you are ready to discuss it. But what about me and how I feel? You refuse to forgive me and move on, but I guess that will always be irrelevant in your eyes. Do you understand that what is of most value in my life besides the love I still have for you is Mikasa and my ability to trust her? I also must feel like I can trust you and the decisions that you make for her in my absence, the self-imposed absence you thrust upon me! I know that she's a good girl and I know that she is special but that doesn't mean that she can ignore my standards for her.'

"Darius, I…

'How can I protect you two if you aren't where you're supposed to be? If we were together now this never would have happened. We could have made this decision together.'

I paused and looked at his weary face. He tried to maintain his scowl and anger but now he just looked sad.

"Darius, listen I apologize for being selfish, but we can't let our stuff spill over in Mikasa's lap. We have to deal with our issues separately, and apart from what's going on with her right now. We dated at sixteen, so you know that we can trust Mikasa. Let's meet this boy so that he understands who she is and who we are. I'm sure that a short conversation with all involved will remedy this situation. And please keep in mind that we were the same age that she is now when you ran your game on me!

That got a smile out of him or more like a smirk.

'I didn't run any game on you woman!'

"Come on Darius; let's put our feelings and his age aside. Right now, I don't think that it matters if he's sixteen or twenty-six. You know as well as I do that men don't mature at the same pace as women and with that in mind you know that it will take a different type of young man to keep Mikasa's interest.

'She isn't seeing this man. I refuse... You say we do not mature as fast, but you do know what a grown man or any boy wants don't you?'

"Yes, in fact I do. A grown man, as you call it, wants the same thing that you wanted right? Please just do us both a favor, don't forbid her from seeing him because if she really likes him, she will find a way and that will lead to her lying to us both. You will lose all that you have built with her, and she will resent you.

Mikasa is beautiful and this is just the first boy, there will be plenty of others interested in her. Don't ruin your relationship with your daughter over a boy that is here today and gone tomorrow.

Darius looked at me and he didn't seem to be buying a word that I was saying, and he was trying his best to hold onto the anger that he came into the house with earlier.

"Okay I don't want to talk about Pooch anymore but since we are on the topics of boys and Mikasa let me ask you this. Were there any other boys that you didn't tell me about and have you spoken to Brandon about giving Mikasa some space from now on, not just this weekend?

I don't want this Pooch around Mikasa, and I don't want Brandon around her anymore either. It's funny and I found out tonight that Brandon kept this boy away from Mikasa for a year and apparently many other boys too. And based on that I'm glad that Brandon held him off for this long but Brandon and Mikasa being together all the time is still not healthy for either one of them, so I'm telling you now Patti, talk to your nephew. I don't like him touching Mikasa all the time and the way that he watches her makes me extremely uncomfortable and angry. I always feel like knocking him out when I see him, but he's your beloved nephew.'

He gave me the look.

'You know that I caught him with his hand on her waist last week. I pulled him to the side, and he acted like he didn't know what I was talking about, but it's inappropriate Patti and if you don't deal with him I will. We've been having this battle for years and I'm sick of it.'

I glanced at him and said, 'Here you go again trying to switch the subject. I will deal with him. Brandon and I will spend some time together this weekend, and I will deal with him then.'

"You do that Patti, and he better not be in your bed either, that big baby!"

'You know that boy never sleeps in my bed. He always…. There you go again. Now, back to the issue at hand. Can we meet Pooch tomorrow? Can you be here at noon?

'Meet him for what Patti? Did you hear me say that I don't want him anywhere near Mikasa? He and his cousin are dealing drugs, and I don't want that element anywhere near our daughter.'

That element? If I'm not mistaken, weren't you a part of that element?

'Wow, really Patti, are you going there? You know that was so far in the past. Why would you mention that now? Can you let that go please?'

"How do you know that he is dealing drugs if you aren't out there?"

'Why are you questioning me like that Patti? I don't have to be involved in something to know what's going down. You're really something else. I've never questioned your integrity but why would I, Miss Prissy? You've never done anything wrong in your life except marry me, right? You're my wife, and you still question my integrity, don't you?

You know what Patti; you can meet him and decide for yourself. I don't want to talk anymore tonight.'

Darius turned and walked away from me slamming the front door. He didn't even think about his jacket that was in the closet and I wanted to go after him, but Mikasa came out of her room and fell in my arms apologizing.

She obviously heard the whole discussion and felt guilty and all that I felt was the sting of my husbands' words and the venom in his voice when he said Miss Prissy. I guess I had finally pushed him away for good.

# CHAPTER FOUR - POOCH

**I feel like I can't move.**

Why am I still out here, standing in the same spot where Mikasa left me?

I'm so pissed that I can't move. I want to call her, need to call her but I don't even have her number.

Where's my cousin! Let me slow down and count to ten to regain my composure. Why did she have to be sixteen? Damn. And her *father,* was moving a lot like her man.

When I looked up Jada and Shane were headed in my direction. Jada was looking around for her friend.

'Where's Mikasa? What did you do with her? Did you scare her off already?'

My cousin was watching my every move. He knew that something wasn't right.

"Jada, I've been asking you about her for months what makes you think that I did something? Her "father" was here."

Jada couldn't contain her shock.

'Her father saw her with you!? Uh oh, what happened?'

"Well, I was about to kiss her again and this man that looked around our age came out of nowhere calling her name. I just knew it was a boyfriend or something until she said Daddy."

'Kiss her, aw no, you were kissing her out here on the street and her dad saw you?'

"Come on, I didn't plan it like that, and I've seen you all hugged up and kissing Shane out here all the time."

'And do you see my father out here hawking? Anyway, what did he do to you?'

I looked at her and I was getting pissed all over again.

"He... she grabbed his arm and tried to drag him down the street away from me. I walked over towards them, but Mikasa asked me to stop. I…

'You didn't! What in the world? Pooch, are you serious, do you know who her father is? You don't want to step to him over Mikasa. You can't win this. People in these streets know him as a man not to be messed with and when it comes to Mikasa, you don't want to try him.'

"I don't think that you understand Jada. I've been waiting almost 13 months just to talk to her, and I finally got the chance to do that today. We ate, talked and you just need to understand that she is for me. I can't explain it, but I just can't stop here. I feel something for her. I can't, just not see her. I am wound up like a watch right now. Where does she live Jada? I need her number."

Jada looked at me like I was crazy and then her phone rang.

'Hello? Slow down Mikasa. What did you say? Wait a minute, he's right here.'

I smiled inside but kept my facial expression as neutral as possible. Before I knew what I was doing, I grabbed Jada's phone and began to walk down the block.

"Mikasa babe, are you okay?"

"'I'm fine. I apologize for leaving you like that, I really didn't want to go. My father was so mad that I didn't want him to speak to you until he calmed down. I know that he meant what he said about me not never, ever seeing you again but my mom sort of convinced him that they should meet you tomorrow, but my dad is still pissed so even though he said that my mom could meet you I don't know if you, I mean we should.'"

"Well, what did your mother say exactly?"

'My father was arguing and fussing about her keeping things from him and my father said something about you dealing. Are you dealing drugs Pooch?'

I laughed and said, "No Mikasa. My cousin Shane does, but I don't. Your father probably saw me out there with him on a few occasions and I've heard about your dad on these streets, but I don't deal drugs, and nothing can stop me from seeing you Mikasa unless you don't want to see me. Do you want to see me?

"'Yes, I want to see you, but I can't betray my father and I can't let this come between my parents. Let me talk to my dad and I will call you back tomorrow.'"

"But you don't have my number. Take it down now and give me yours after you write this. And put my name down there too, Darius Jackson, my number is (718) ***-5696, and my address is 3042 Carpenter Avenue, Bronx, New York 10656. My birthday is ...."

"'Okay don't be funny and don't tell me that your real name is Darius?'"

"Yes why? Was that your last boyfriends' name?"

"'I already told you that I never had a boyfriend. That's my fathers' name. I had to laugh. Imagine me meeting a guy like you with the same name as my father. I mean, how unlikely is that? Well anyway I apologize again for what happened. My Dad can be so unreasonable at times.'"

"You don't have to apologize Mikasa but what do you mean by a guy like me? You do believe me when I say that I don't sell drugs don't you? I have a business and I go to Hunter College. I also invest in and own property. I'm a stand-up guy. I had to make my parents proud, you know."

"'I didn't mean it like that Pooch I just meant; I mean someone that I'm attracted to that is all.'"

She hesitated then said, 'My father reacted the way that he did because he has never seen me so interested in anyone and your age bothers him although I never even told him your age. I am sure that he thinks that you are older than you are.

Part of the problem with this is that I've been so sheltered that my father just can't seem to handle the fact that I'm growing up. I've spent my whole life hanging out just with my cousin Brandon and clearly, I should have dated someone before this.

I 'm graduating from high school soon and I've never been out on a date with a boy. I bet that you never had to meet the parents and be interrogated before dating a girl, have you?'"

"Honestly, I haven't, but I don't have a problem with that, I just never had to wait so long to meet a girl either but so far, I feel as if it was worth it to finally spend some time with you and I can't turn back now."

"'I feel the same way. I mentioned you to my mom a couple of days ago, so she was trying to give me the space to socialize. She wants me to feel comfortable on my own when I go away to college. So, meeting a boy and possibly dating was something that she could deal with but of course my father doesn't want me to date, doesn't want me to go away to college, he just doesn't want me to grow up period. Can you imagine that he's contemplating leasing a place near my school so that he can take care of me while I'm there?

My Mom has been going at it with him; fighting him for my freedom and of course I love her for it, but I feel so guilty for what he's putting her through now and I found out some things about him and why they separated tonight that I wasn't aware of before.

Oh, my goodness; why am I telling you all of this and I just met you? Just take down my number and call me tomorrow. Let me talk to my dad and try to work this out with them.'"

"Mikasa, you don't have to feel funny about talking to me about anything. I'm glad that you feel comfortable talking to me like this. And I really want to see you tomorrow, but I will wait for your call."

"'I will work on that as soon as I get off the phone Pooch. Call me tomorrow all, right?'"

"Alright Mikasa. "

I couldn't help but smile as Jada approached me to retrieve her phone. I said good night to Mikasa and handed Jada her phone.

'So, I guess that all is right in your world now?' Jada replied.

"Not quite but it will be. See you later Jada. Shane, I will get with you later man, one.

## DARIUS

I drove around for over an hour trying to clear my head. My phone was going off and I knew it was Mikasa, so I just let it continue to go to voicemail. I couldn't talk to my daughter or my wife because I felt like I would say things to them that I could never take back. I wanted to hate Patti so badly and blame her for all that was going on, but it continued to tear at my heart that we weren't together. I always felt like she thought of herself as the better parent, and it seemed so easy for her to edge me out of a decision that had the potential to change our daughters' life forever. I felt like I didn't matter to her anymore and it really hurt me deep in a place that I thought that I couldn't feel anymore.

When I pulled up to the house, I thought that I saw Patti's' car but I chalked it up to wishful thinking. I thought about the Hennessy that I had in the house, and I knew that I would indulge. I opened the door and there was a light on in the kitchen. I put my hand in the closet preparing myself to do damage to whoever was in my house. I stood still and gazed in the mirror at the shadow in the distance.

'Darius is that you?'

It was my wife's voice. I exhaled.

"What are you doing here Patti?"

I sighed but inside my heart was glad. I slipped the protection back into the closet and closed the door before she appeared in front of me. She had on a nice raincoat and of course she looked good but what did it matter?

'Darius, can we talk?'

"I am tired of talking Patti. No matter what I say, you just do what you want to do anyway so really what's the point."

'Well, the point is that I still love you so much Darius and you need to know that. I really want to clear the air with you and lay it all out there. I didn't realize that you still felt like I judge you for the mistake that you made so long ago. I also didn't know that I was Miss Prissy to you. I thought that you loved the fact that I'm so feminine and as you say prissy. I thought that you liked having a woman who knows how to carry herself and is very selective. I thought that being a lady and setting a good example for our daughter by being respectable and striving for excellence…. I thought that you loved having an honorable wife.'

"Patti don't play with me. Miss Prissy doesn't refer to your character; it refers to your judgment. All the things you just said, you know that I love all those things about you. The thing that I don't like is you judging me for making one mistake. I left your house tonight because I didn't want to say hurtful things to you out of anger, so I apologize if calling you Miss Prissy hurt your feelings."

'We all make mistakes; I know that Darius but that one mistake you made so many years ago, could've cost me my license and landed both of us in jail leaving Mikasa in foster care! Listen I didn't come here to rehash all of this or to argue I want to apologize.'

Patti opened her coat and all I saw was black lace.

"So, I like what I see, in fact I love what I see but is that all that you have for me Patti because I'm not biting this time. As good as you look and as much as I want you it's unfair to me that every time that we have a disagreement you use your body to make up with me and then you are back in your own bed and business as usual after everything is resolved. If you aren't willing to discuss us getting back together right here, right now I don't want you throwing me a bone anymore. If I can't have all of you all the time, I don't want any of you. I'm so tired of feeling broken and empty without you." He paused but I was afraid to speak. He continued.

"And I guess you're horny tonight, but I need more than that, so much more."

She went to slap me, but I caught her hand and turned her towards the living room. I held her right in front of me and said, "If you really came here to talk to me, please close your coat and have a seat in the living room."

She had the nerve to get upset and she grabbed her keys and headed for the door.

"Patti, if you really love me like you just said button your coat and have a seat; don't be difficult."

She glared at me long and hard and then she went over to the couch and sat crossing her arms to hold the coat closed. The keys were still in her hand.

 I took my jacket off and poured myself a drink. I offered her one also, but she refused. I took a seat across from her wondering how we had gotten to this point.

 She looked straight ahead and said, 'I never meant to hurt you Darius and I apologize for making you feel like I'm judging you. I was so angry when I discovered that you weren't the perfect man that I thought you were. I was also hurt that you didn't confide in me about what you had done instead of letting my sister destroy me with the revelation.

When she confronted me about it, I couldn't even play it off because you didn't tell me. I denied it and cursed her for it but come to find out that she was right about you. About what you did.

When that happened to us, you caught dealing; I never wanted to separate from you, but I was so afraid to lose our child and all that I worked for just because you had other ideas about how to support us. I never meant to be selfish, and you know, I never should have let you pay for my education either. Now I don't accept any of the blame for your decision to do what you did but I should've taken that responsibility from you when we separated, and I should've worked my way through medical school so that you wouldn't think of me as an ungrateful wife who used you.

I understand that you're angry with me, and you're hurt but don't you realize that I can't love anyone else but you? You said that I was selfish, but I didn't think that I could trust you again or know how to put us back together even though I missed you so much. During the time that we were apart I toyed with the idea of dating this doctor a couple of years ago because I figured that you and I wouldn't get back together but I couldn't. I just couldn't. My heart wouldn't allow it. I mean besides the fact that we are still married I just couldn't stop thinking about you and how I still loved you I mean still love you. I want to get back together with you Darius I just figured that once Mikasa went to Vassar we could talk about it and try to make it work again.'

"So, wait, you were going to date someone while you were still married to me?"

'Aww come on Darius we have been separated for eleven years! Why are you giving me such a hard time tonight?

"I'm giving you a hard time!? Really?"

'Really, I just can't say anything right to you! On several occasions throughout the eleven years, you bragged to me in detail about dating other women and now that I mention one date you want to act like I committed a federal crime?'

"It is a crime because you broke up with me Patti, I didn't leave you! The separation and you leaving my bed empty every night; that was your idea.

After a while I thought that you were never going to get back with me too so I figured that somehow my dating other women would snap you back to your senses but you, you always could take me or leave me. You knew that I was dating another woman and that didn't elicit any response from you, good or bad. I expected you to tell me to stop, to yell at me or protest but you just listened and acted as if you were pleased that I was dating instead of letting me know that it bothered you.

I needed you, Patti; I needed your attention, your love, your company or at least to make you jealous enough to fight for me, but you didn't, so I continued to fill that need for you with other women, but it never worked for me. Never.

No matter who I saw or what I did I was still on your doorstep every day. And after all of that and knowing that you caused us to be apart you have the nerve to tell me that you contemplated dating a man instead of just letting me know that you wanted me back. I mean I've been at your house *every day* and we talk on the phone *every day*. You say that you love me today, here, now but why couldn't you show me that you still loved me then by telling me that?"

'Listen to me Darius and hear me clearly. I love you and I've always loved you so much that all that I could think about when we started dating was you and all that I wanted to do every day was see you. That's how our relationship started and that's how it stopped.

The day that you left our home, I felt as if I was on the verge of a nervous breakdown, and I'm sure that my sister was just counting the days until she heard or saw that I had finally lost my mind and was on the street babbling to myself.

Every night after putting Mikasa to bed I would cry in the shower and cry myself to sleep. I felt like a functioning zombie. I went to work every day, but I was not myself and my parents called me every day telling me to come home. They wanted to care for me, and the baby, and they wanted me to divorce you but as angry and distraught as I was that was something that I just couldn't do. I loved you and I never knew anything else but loving you so even though I had to leave you I didn't leave you in my heart. I thought that if you learned the lesson the hard way by losing us you would get yourself together. Days and months passed, and I still didn't know if I could ever really trust you. You came by every afternoon and you were always amazing with Mikasa but I had nightmares about you going to jail and having our child taken away so I said to myself I will just wait to reconcile with you when she was older so if anything happened, God forbid my parents could raise her and at least Mikasa would remember that once upon a time she had parents who loved her.

The bottom line now is that I know I can never make up for all the pain that I caused you. All that we can do today is move forward and you have to believe and trust that I love you just as much as you love me. And I do love you, Darius. I miss your kiss, the constant attention, the way you spoil me, being in your arms every night. I could go on and on, but I just want you to understand that the only reason that I didn't tell you that I wanted you back is that I didn't want…I was still afraid to trust you and I guess that I didn't want you to reject me. I was afraid that you would.'

"You must be kidding Patti? Despite all that we have been through, how could I ever reject you? You and Mikasa are my life and why do you think I was hanging around all the time? And I asked you to get back with me every day during the first year that we were apart.'

'Yes, you did but after that year you stopped asking and then you started dating so I thought that you were done with me.'

"I don't want to be difficult, but I have to say that it would have felt so good if you just told me that you wanted me back. I mean you know how much I love you. I would've appreciated hearing that from you Patti."

'Well, I will say it now. I do want you back in my life as my husband, my lover and my friend and I forgive you. If you want me back in your life, I am prepared to do whatever I have to do to be with you.'

"Sounds good Patti but I have to think about it. I sat back in my chair, my arms folded with a big Kool Aid smile on my face. You know that you will have to do a lot to make it all up to me. You know that don't you? Eleven years is a long time."

'I smirked at him and said, 'whatever you want me to do I will do Darius just say that we can be together again'.

"So why didn't you call me?"

'Darius!'

"Yes, I want you back and we can be together but please understand that you have eleven years' worth of making up to do. I mean, I want five-star royal treatment. You must treat me better than you did before."

'Okay.'

"I want massages every night, from head to toe. I want you to feed me my dinner from my plate and yours and I want you to rub my feet when I come out of the shower every night like I used to do for you."

'All right.'

"And ….

'Come on Darius, I will do whatever you want me to do but we still have other issues to discuss. Now that the real thing that was eating at you has been resolved can you agree to meet Mikasa's friend later today so that we can try to see why she is interested in him?'

"Why didn't you call me woman?"

'Darius, stop asking me that and answer the question.'

"We don't need to meet him because I already know him. I know that Mikasa is on Jada's block every Friday like clockwork with Brandon in tow. I know that he has been there also, watching her from a distance. I know that he and the other one was standing around on the streets as if they had nothing better to do and I could tell that he had a thing for our daughter because he was always telling the other one something every time that he saw Mikasa. I saw him talking to Jada at length after Mikasa left each Friday, so I've been over there every other week checking on her welfare."

'Darius, are you spying on our child?'

"What do you mean am I spying on our child? She is my daughter and I know how it is on Fordham Road. I don't want her there at all but since Jada lives there and I understand that she wants to see her friend I need to see Mikasa in the girl's surroundings and zero in on whoever is trying to get at my child. And don't worry she doesn't even know that I'm around.

Do you remember Eddie from Tremont, the short dark-skinned cat? Well, he has an apartment facing the front of Fordham Hill, so I go by and see him from time to time and sit in his window to see who hangs out there. Every Friday without fail I see this man Pooch out there with a couple of other guys but specifically with the cat that I know sells drugs. I have been by there on other days just to see what was up and I saw him asking Jada for something on several occasions, but I could tell that he was not into her. Then on one occasion when Brandon was with Jada, and Mikasa I saw Pooch watching Mikasa and trying to approach her. As cool as she was from a distance it was obvious to me that she was interested in him also, but Brandon wasn't letting him get anywhere near Mikasa.

Just trust me when I say this, I have seen him, and I'm telling you that he is not the one for Mikasa. And anyway, I thought that we wanted her to wait until she was eighteen to date."

'You wanted her to wait Darius not we and honestly you are being unrealistic with that. Do you realize that she is graduating at the top of her class, and you will not allow her to go on a date? Our *reasonable* expectation was for her to date when she graduated from high school. She is sixteen and she is graduating so please be fair.'

"Be fair; be reasonable, you're so demanding of me tonight! I think that it is fair for me to check any man out that is interested in my, our daughter. But for now, I will tell you what you want to hear and officially get him out of the way of our daughter. We can meet him here at my house at noon. End of that discussion. Now, are you staying with me tonight? Think about it for a minute and be fair and reasonable."

I looked at him and we both laughed.

'I will stay for a while, but I won't feel comfortable going home in the morning in my raincoat. I don't have any clothes here.'

"Nobody told you to come over here in the middle of the night in your underwear."

And that was my cue, so I opened my coat and let it drop to floor and Darius got up from his seat to meet me.

'Well, I don't see anybody complaining.'

## POOCH

About an hour later after showering and getting comfortable in my room I called Mikasa. 'Hello?'

"Hi Pooch." I could hear her smile through the phone.

'Did I wake you up?'

"Of course not, I was lying here listening to Dru Hill thinking about you. I've been calling my father for the last hour and a half, and it continues to go to voicemail. I went to speak to my mother about you and she left a note saying that she was going to see my dad. I feel so bad about that because I told my mom about you and planned to see you and my gut told me to tell my dad, but I didn't because I figured that he would throw a monkey wrench in my plan. Now because of that my parents were arguing, and my dad was accusing my mom of keeping things from him. My plan for as long as I can remember has been to get them back together and I seem to be pushing them further apart."

'How long have they been separated?'

"Since I was about four years old."

'Wow, that is long, but don't worry about it Mikasa. If you just continue to be patient things are going to work out with your parents and with us. I know that our situation doesn't compare to how long your parents have been apart but I waited this long to talk to you so I can wait a little longer to see you again and it seems like you're doing all that you can to make it happen so whenever they agree I will be there.'

"That sounds good Pooch, but I can't stop thinking about it. I have never ever seen my father get as upset as he was tonight. I mean, he rarely gets upset about anything except over my cousin Brandon and I don't like him to be upset with me.

So now can you imagine what I have done to the progress of them getting back together? They have been separated for so long now, but you would think that it just happened yesterday. I wish that they would just forget what happened with me today, forgive each other and get back together. If we still lived together as a family, this would have never happened.'

"What exactly happened with your parents if you don't mind me asking?"

'They don't like to talk about it, but I heard some things tonight that I didn't know, and I really don't feel comfortable sharing any of it. It's just too shocking to me, and I would like to talk to my father about it first.'

"I can understand that. Just know that if you ever want to talk about anything, it doesn't matter what it is, you can talk to me. And not to completely change the subject but I just couldn't stop thinking about you. I couldn't sleep; I didn't want to watch TV and didn't want to eat so I just had to call and hear your voice. And it's blowing my mind that you're only sixteen. I really didn't think that I would be attracted to a sixteen-year-old at this point in my life. You're something else girl.

Mikasa laughed and said, 'And I didn't think that I would be so attracted to a grown man as my father says it. He had the nerve to tell my mother that you were practically his age.'

Well, when he approached us, I just knew that he was your man. He really looks too young to be your father.

'I know, but please don't ever tell him that. He hates it when we are out together, and people think that I'm his girlfriend and lately now that I am older, he gets the comments and winks all the time whenever we are out. I think that it is funny, but he gets so pissed. And if you think that he looks young just wait until you see my mother. We easily pass for sisters now that I'm older.'

So, your father thinks I'm in my late twenties? Do I look that old to you?

'Very funny, of course not. But he knows that you're not sixteen and I thought that you were seventeen at the most. I know that he was just trying to get a rise out of my mother for letting me see you in the first place and he obviously isn't in his late twenties if he has me. You know the thing with my dad is that he still sees me as his baby. I really regret not showing much interest in boys before now. If I did, my father would have been over this phase by now. I mean he doesn't even trust my cousin Brandon around me, and he's a baby. My father is really extra.'

Is Brandon the shadow that you always had with you every time that I saw you?

I laughed. 'Yes, that's Brandon.'

I don't know him, but I have to say that just like your father, I don't trust him either.

'Well, why would you say that?'

You don't remember? The first time that we saw each other I came towards you, and he immediately blocked me before I said anything. And when Jada introduced us, he still didn't move and every time after that he had his arm around your neck, or he was holding your hand or your arm. He was sending the message that you were taken without you even being aware of it and if you remember, he wouldn't even let me get close enough to talk to you without him being between us. It also didn't help that Jada neglected to introduce him as your cousin but eventually after she saw that I wouldn't be discouraged about him or anyone else she let me know that he was your cousin. I didn't believe her though because his body language said differently. That's why I say I don't trust him I mean; I don't want to agree with your dad, to spite you but he may have a point here.

'Oh, so since I am a girl, I can't see that my own cousin is attracted to me. I know that he has a crush on me but that's all that it is. I am his only cousin, and we are both only children, so we're tight. He's at my house all the time, so I'm really all that he knows. As he gets older, I'm sure that he will outgrow it.'

Outgrow it, how old is he now? You both look eighteen to me.

'He's fourteen.'

Fourteen! Are you kidding me? He is practically as tall as me and what is he about two hundred or two hundred twenty pounds?

'Yeah, he is 6'2' and about 210 pounds.'

Is he over there now?

I laughed again. 'Come on no he isn't.'

I just asked because you said that you were home alone. I don't want to have to come over there and check him.

I was laughing again. 'You're too much Pooch. I'm glad that you called though I really couldn't get to sleep.'

I couldn't sleep either. You know when you touched me in the restaurant my whole body felt different.

'Stop playing. Are you trying to run game on me now?'

I'm so serious. I don't know if it was the anticipation of seeing or being with you, but I felt something and then you kissed me and, I…. I can't tell you all this so soon. You might think that I'm crazy.

'Why would I think that if you're telling me the truth?'

I don't know but I will say this. You said that you were sheltered earlier, and I'm so glad that you were. I mean if you weren't someone else would have had your heart by now and we wouldn't be talking to each other like this. Everything is happening the way that it did because we're supposed to be together. I like you Mikasa. I don't know how many ways to say it and I don't know yet how I will convince your father about it, but I could never take advantage of you. He needs to know that.

'You know you are saying these things to me as I'm lying in my bed, and I feel like you're right here with me. Your words feel like… like you are here right in front of me, speaking to me.

You think that my father needs to know how we feel about each other, but I suspect that he already senses the intensity of it. He knows that……do you know what, scratch that thought and let me just say good night before I tell you everything that there is to say about us and how I feel before we even have our first date. I hope to see you tomorrow. Goodnight.'

Good night babe.

'His words warmed my heart, and I didn't think that I would, but I fell right asleep with a smile on my face.

## MIKASA

I don't know when my mother came in or how long I slept but she was in my room talking to me as if I were awake already. My mother sat on the edge of my chaise tapping me lightly on the shoulder.

'Mikasa baby wake up! I spoke to your father, and he said that we could meet your friend. It is ten o'clock now and he wants us to meet at the house at noon. Wake up baby and give him a call.'

Huh? Good morning, Mommy, how are you?

I heard her clearly, but I wanted her to repeat what she just said.

'Call Pooch and give him your dad's address so that he can meet us there at noon. I know that you heard me the first time so get up and get it cracking.'

She popped me on the leg and left the room humming a tune. I couldn't remember her being in such a good mood so early on a Saturday morning. I texted Pooch and he was calling me midway through completing the message.

"Good morning beautiful."

Hi, how are you?

"I'm awesome."

Where are you? I hear noise in the background.

"At the car wash getting the car detailed. It's part of my Saturday routine. After this I'm heading to the diner for a bite to eat."

Well could you meet us at my dads' house at noon today?

"Hold up Mikasa, say that again. What are you saying to me?"

I'm saying write down my fathers' address and meet us there at twelve. I have to get up and get dressed now so I will see you there.

"Alright, you aren't playing, are you?"

Pooch! I will see you soon.

"Okay Mikasa see you at noon."

Across town Pooch was pulling out in his A8L smelling like black cherry and looking as hot as ever with his ride glistening in the sun. After leaving the diner and the florist he leaned over in his ride and punched in the address.

I walked into my mothers' room and started hitting her with questions.

What did you do and say to make Daddy change his mind? What did he say? What did you say? Is he still upset with you? Did my dad really sell drugs? Is that why you left him? When did you get in last night or did you get in last night?

'Mikasa stop with the questions and get ready. We can talk about all this another time. We are going to sit down together and see what this boy is about and if your father still doesn't like him, we will have to find a way to deal with that together. Do you understand me?'

Yes, I understand. Thanks Mom.

"Don't thank me yet just go get ready."

She smiled at me, and I turned and went into the bathroom. I splashed my face with water and turned on the shower. I lathered up repeatedly with the Almond Cookie body wash, rinsed off and stepped out of the shower. I applied the Almond Cookie crème generously over my entire body, dressed and did my hair. I had on a pair of the jeans my mother purchased a few weeks ago, a lavender, beige, and purple silk Pucci top and lavender leather Italian sandals that Daddy bought for me. I stepped into the living room and my mother looked beautiful in her sea green, peach and white halter top and white jeans. She wore higher heels just like mine in peach. They were also a gift from Daddy, and they were also straight from Italy.

He loved to shop for us but the only gifts that my mother accepted from him were the shoes that Daddy always sent through me.

I entered the kitchen and said, 'Thanks again Mom for this outfit. I love it.'

I also loved the fact that my mom was just as hip and pretty as she was.

I drank the glass of fresh juice that she made me, and we headed for the door as she grabbed her keys and her Louis purse. We left the house at about eleven twenty and as we pulled up in front of Dad's house my phone was ringing.

From the car window I could see that Pooch was parked across from my dad's house in the prettiest navy Audi that I ever saw. He got out when he saw us pull up and I waved at him. Mom parked and I got out. Pooch spoke to me then introduced himself to my mother saying how nice it was to meet her.

'It's nice to meet you too Pooch but what is your real name, the name that your mother gave you?'

He smiled and said, 'My name is Darius.'

'Well, isn't that something? Your Dad will get a kick out of that Mikasa. Let's go inside.'

As we turned towards my fathers' door Pooch reached into his back seat and brought out some flowers and a shopping bag from the diner. I looked at him and smiled and he spoke.

"Mrs. Jones these are for you. He handed her a bunch of white Calla Lilies wrapped like a bridal bouquet in cellophane."

'How very nice of you, they are beautiful.'

He spoke again and handed me the prettiest purple Tulips wrapped the same way.

"These are for you Mikasa. I don't know what you like yet, but I figured that the prettiest flower that they had would make you smile."

They are beautiful. Thank you, Pooch!

'I also brought breakfast. I was on my way to diner when Mikasa called so I figured that everyone might like something.'

I thanked him again as my mom smiled and rang the doorbell. She looked through the window as she pulled out her key saying, 'Where is your father?'

It was about eleven forty-five and my dad pulled up as soon as we got the door open.

Pooch brought the stuff inside and headed back out of the door running straight into my father. Pooch was about an inch shorter than my dad. He stepped back and said,

'Excuse me and good morning Mr. Jones, how are you?'

My father looked at Pooch then looked at his watch and said, 'Hello, I see that you made it.'

Pooch replied, 'Yes I did, extended his hand and said, I'm Darius, Darius Jackson, thank you for having me here sir.'

My mother and I glanced at my father at the same time, and he just smirked.

"Your name is Darius, and you think that's funny, don't you Mikasa?'

My mother and I smiled at the same time, and she said, 'Now we both have a Darius.'

My father frowned at the comment and shook his head at my mother as if to say, no she doesn't.

Pooch continued to hold his hand out until dad finally shook it.

'I didn't have the opportunity to introduce myself to you properly last night and I apologize to you both for that. You should know that I like your daughter, I would love to date her, I didn't know her age until yesterday and I just turned nineteen.'

My father was frowning again and said, "Okay why don't we all sit down and talk."

I sat next to Pooch on one side of the table as my parents sat on the other.

Pooch handed me a box of Italian Chocolate Truffles and grabbed my hand to hold it.

Daddy noticed the gesture and said to my mother, 'Don't you two look nice. The complimented rested well between us but in the same tone my father remarked, 'Pooch you can take your hand off of my daughter because I haven't decided if you can date or touch her yet.' Respectfully, Pooch removed his hand from mine.

Daddy's comment was full of sarcasm, and he clearly wasn't pleased that my mother and I were glammed up like we were going out on a date. Pooch looked at us and said, 'Yes you both look very nice,' causing my father to glare at him briefly.

My mother touched my dad to ease his gaze from Pooch. She got up to get some plates and she put the bagels, donut holes, and muffins on the table along with the containers of green tea and fresh orange juice. I got up to help her with the glasses and bring the napkins. When we were all seated again my mother spoke.

"Darius, I understand that you and my daughter were kissing outside of Jimmy's last night. My husband and I are not happy about that. I, we, need to know who you are and what motivated you to make a move on our baby right outside on the street like that. It is my understanding that yesterday was the first time the two of you have spoken at length, so you need to understand whose daughter you are dealing with and what we expect of her. We trust Mikasa and know that she doesn't make a practice of kissing boys in the street.

Daddy interrupted and said, 'Man; she was kissing a man.'

Mom continued. Mikasa is not a common or average girl. We raised her with certain standards, and she must be respected by whoever she decides to date. The other issue to address right away is that my husband believes that you are a street hustler and that is not acceptable for our daughter.

Pooch wasted no time and spoke immediately.

'Mr. and Mrs. Jones I had no intention of disrespecting your daughter. I was, …let me apologize first for kissing her in public. I didn't intend on doing that but after we ate… Let me back up a bit to properly explain. I was surprised to see Mikasa get off the bus yesterday afternoon and I was even more surprised that her and Jada were alone, no cousin in sight. So, I approached her respectfully and finally got to speak to her. At that moment I didn't expect to feel anything, but I did. Mikasa let me take her to eat, or should I say, we walked to the restaurant together, we talked and laughed and something that I can't explain happened. There is something about Mikasa. I saw your daughter for the first time over a year ago and I had been patiently waiting just to have a conversation with her because it was clear to me then that she wasn't common by any stretch of the imagination. After talking to her for just a minute I felt that, so you don't have to worry about me thinking that she's common. I also understand that you have standards. I have them also. If you give me a chance you will see that I'm a good guy. I'm a year away from obtaining my B.S. in Psychology at Hunter College. I started taking college courses in my junior year of high school, so I was halfway at the goal of obtaining this degree by the time I graduated from high school. I own two Fitness Centers in the Bronx; I have two homes and my investment portfolio is extensive. I have something of value to offer your daughter besides my good looks, charm, and personality. I'm not a street hustler now nor have I ever been. I socialize on occasion with my cousin Shane and that is his lifestyle, but I can drastically limit the time that I spend with him if it's going to hinder my ability to see Mikasa.

I would like to date Mikasa, and I just turned nineteen last month, so I'm not that old. I understand that she just turned sixteen and is graduating from high school this year and believe me, I didn't know or expect to date a sixteen-year-old at my age, but Mikasa is different. She seems so mature and advanced that I know that we could be a great match for each other."

Pooch continued to look my father directly in the eye and said, 'I assure you that I'm not involved in any way with my cousin's business. He's my only cousin in New York so I do see him from time to time but as of today his time with me in Mikasa's presence will be extremely limited or none at all.'

Mom looked at Daddy then back at Pooch. She was waiting for him to say something and finally he did.

'What are your parents like, what do they do?'

"They don't do anything anymore. They were killed about fourteen months ago in a car accident. My mother was a nurse, and my father was an engineer who also owned a software company."

My mom sighed and apologized to Darius for his loss and my father did the same.

'What about siblings?'

I'm an only child. My grandparents and all my cousins besides Shane live down south.

'You said that you attend Hunter College, right? What's your GPA?'

"Darius, you must be kidding! He just wants to date Mikasa not marry her. Are we talking to him or interviewing him for a position?"

'Listen here Patti you wanted to meet him, so I need to know everything about him. Mikasa will be a double major at Vassar. Do you think she will be free to study and achieve like she has all of her life if her "boyfriend" has a C average? Please remember that this is about Mikasa, not about his feelings about me and my questions. Please continue Pooch.'

I'm an honor roll student, my GPA is 3.94, and I am graduating Magna Cum Laude next year. After graduation, I will continue my studies and obtain my master's.

'And what about your health do you have tuberculosis, hepatitis or any other airborne disease that I should know about?'

My mom and I gave him a look, but he didn't hesitate to answer.

I'm very healthy, Mr. Jones. In fact, I see my doctor twice a year as a precaution because I work out vigorously and consistently and I like to keep an eye on all my levels. I'm disease-free including STD's. I'm 6'4", two hundred and twenty pounds, I eat right as often as possible, and I love to travel.

Pooch said it all with a smile and I liked that he was keeping up with my dad. Dad was about to ask another question when Mom interrupted.

"Well, it seems as if my husband has forgotten what it's like to date. You seem like a nice young man, note the word seem but I don't have a problem with you dating Mikasa. You're nineteen and she is sixteen but that's not a problem either as long as you are respectful. Darius and I were Mikasa's age when…

Now my father cleared his throat, interrupted, and gave my mother the look.

'Patti, he doesn't need to know all of that and listen young man, I love my wife and I love my daughter and it seems as though they have endorsed you here today, but I have not. If you want to DATE my daughter, you have to come through me. I need to know everything about you before she gets in a car and goes anywhere with you. You answered every question here today correctly, but I need to get a feel for who you really are inside. I only have one child; one daughter and I am just not comfortable handing my daughter over to the first man that asks for her."

'I respect that Mr. Jones and I am willing to do whatever you ask but what if the first man is the best man?'

That made my father pause. "If you are *the best man,* which shouldn't even be a consideration for a sixteen-year-old, you will have to prove it to me first. And just for the record, dumping all your feelings for my daughter out on me like vomit really isn't the best way to get on my good side.

Take my card. This is the key to seeing my daughter, so whenever you want to see Mikasa plan to see me first. We have to share more than a name for you to impress me.'

My mother sighed as I sat expressionless wanting to shrink right under my seat. Daddy got up like he was leaving, and Pooch stood up too.

'Well, may I set up our first date now because I would like to see Mikasa this evening?'

For the first time in my life, I saw my father close his eyes, sigh, and say yes, all in the same breath.

Inside I was smiling as my mother glanced at me. Pooch touched my hand, said that he would call me later and followed my father to the door. He said goodbye to my mother; she thanked him again for the flowers and food then my mom and I packed everything back up and headed out of the door.

# Chapter 5 - BRANDON

It was about 2pm and Auntie was nowhere in sight. As I sat in the living room watching the game, I heard the door. My Aunt and Mikasa entered the house, set down their bags and flowers and I smiled. Mikasa waved at me and went to her room.

My aunt said, 'Hey Brandon, how are you? Are you ready to go to Home Depot so that we can pick up some things?

I looked towards Mikasa's room for a moment, said yes and reluctantly followed my aunt out of the house. We got to the store and after picking up a plethora of items we left the store. I packed everything into the trunk of the car, then got in besides my aunt.

'Are you hungry?'

You know it Auntie. 'Let's get Italian. I feel like Shrimp Parmesan.'

My aunt called ahead to her favorite restaurant and when we arrived, they began to bring our dishes out and place them on the table. When everything was set out and the food was blessed, we began to eat.

After a few bites, my aunt said, 'you know that I love you, don't you? You are the son that I never had and Mikasa loves you like a brother.

I nodded in agreement.

You also know that you and Mikasa are always together, which is great but after your prom, you need to give her some space.'

I was looking at my aunt now, a bit disoriented, but I continued to eat.

'She can't babysit you anymore. She will be off to college soon and dating. It's just time for both of you to spread your wings a bit and hang out more with just your group of friends.'

Babysit Auntie, really? I am fourteen years old. Did she say that she babysits me? I am bigger than her and I take care of her more than she takes care of me.

'No, she didn't say baby sit I'm saying that she is babysitting you. Mikasa wants to date now and hang out with Jada without taking you everywhere with her. Having her younger cousin around all the time is not such a good look for her, and what about your friends? When do you see them?'

Date? Who does Mikasa want to date? I have never seen Mikasa with any boy. Date?

'That is my point boy. How could you see any boy with her when you are always around? The boy that I met today thought that you were her boyfriend because he always sees you with her. And I'm sure that other boys thought the same and stayed away too.'

What boy Auntie? What are you saying? I can't hang out with my cousin anymore. What boy?

I was getting agitated now because I wasn't happy about another man coming between me and Mikasa.

'Brandon calm down, get a hold of yourself and don't raise your voice at me in this restaurant. I'm trying to have a civil conversation with you, you need to hear what I'm saying and stop reacting like this.'

Aunt Patti was looking at me, clearly disturbed at my outburst and I was embarrassed and mad as heck.

'Brandon, we're family and that's not going to change. We will always be family but in a few months Mikasa will be in college. You will not see her every day anymore. Next year you will be at Duke. It's time for you to hang out with your friends and prepare for that time away. Nothing will ever change how we feel about you, but you need to fall back some. You're not Mikasa's Daddy, and you definitely aren't her boyfriend either. You need to have interests and friends of your own. You understand that don't you?'

But Aunt Patti, who is always there to protect Mikasa? Who covers her when boys are coming on too strong from every direction? Who takes care of and cooks for her every weekend?

She's my best friend and I know that I'm not her Daddy or her boyfriend. I just…

"Listen, I'm not debating with you on this. Stop picking Mikasa up every day from school and stop showing up everywhere that she hangs out. You can still come over to the house of course but stay out of Mikasa's bedroom unless she calls you in there do you hear me?'

Auntie, I …

'Do you hear me boy?'

Okay Aunt Patti, okay, but please don't treat me like my mother does. Please. She pushed me away and on you and no one is ever home at my house. I don't care about having friends and I like spending all my time with Mikasa. If I stop picking Mikasa up every day I have to go to my empty house, and you know that my mother doesn't cook or spend any time with me there, and she isn't interested in my grades or anything else about me. You want me to stop hanging out with Mikasa but without her I would go crazy! Nobody loves me but you and Mikasa so what am I supposed to do with myself now?

I watched the melodrama unfold and folded my arms across my chest. 'I just said that you can continue to come to my house, but you're fourteen, you're handsome, and it seems as if you're immensely popular at school. Start socializing with people your own age who aren't related to you. It's not healthy for you or Mikasa to be with each other exclusively all the time.'

The check came and I reached for it.

'Brandon stop playing with me; I will pay the bill. You're not that grown, and this isn't a date. Save your money for hanging out with your girlfriend Kim. Isn't that her name? Why aren't you spending your time with her?'

Yes, that's her name but she… she isn't what I expected her to be. We never really hang out because she's only interested in coming to the house to have sex all the time. She's so fast. She's pretty but she can't stay out of my bed.

'Your bed? Are you saying what I think that you're saying? Are you sexually active already Brandon?'

Auntie!

'Don't Auntie me, you are only fourteen years old Brandon and how old is she?'

She is seventeen and turns eighteen next month.

'What! Does your mother know…. oh, never mind. Why are you dating a seventeen-year-old girl Brandon?'

Because I can Auntie, 'I said and smiled. I chose her. I don't have any time for girls my age. Too silly, too immature for me. I like older girls like Mikasa's age at least.

'So, are you telling me that because you can you do? Does that apply to stealing and lying? Does it also apply to cheating on exams and doing any other unlawful or ungodly thing because you can?'

Oh, come on Auntie, I'm not saying all of that. I know right from wrong but why should I date a fourteen-year-old freshman when I can date a 17-year-old senior? Grown women come on to me all the time but my limit right now is seventeen.

'Well why stop there if you can? You come to church every Sunday with me, and you hear about saving yourself for marriage and you know that you are called and set apart to be holy just like God intends for it to be, like Mikasa and I. I know that we haven't really discussed this before but what makes you think that you don't have to abide by the Word of God?'

What I heard at church is that women are supposed to save themselves for marriage. Whenever I've seen anyone go up to the altar for the purity pledge at our church it has been all girls. You never ever see boys go up there. And no one in the church has called us on it. So, when I hear one thing and see another, I live by what I see. I know that Mikasa made a vow to save herself for marriage, but I didn't make that vow and you never said anything about it to me until now.

'So, what about your conscience Brandon? Does it feel right to you as a fourteen-year-old boy having sex in your mothers' apartment?'

So now the issue is respecting my mothers' home? Well then to be honest Auntie I don't feel one way or another about having sex in that house. My mother does it all the time and she doesn't care if I know it. I don't mean to be disrespectful to you but as I said earlier, I do what I see. Now of course I can't deny that I see how you live and how you are raising Mikasa, but you don't have a son, so I don't see how your lifestyle affects who I sleep with. I also don't have a father to show me a different way. Uncle Darius doesn't even talk to me much about anything so what do you expect from me? My mother doesn't care, doesn't ask, and doesn't complain and besides, I'm clean, and she would not notice that I was having sex if she ever looked. I clean the house between the weekly visits from the cleaning service.

I sat back stunned by the conversation that I was having with my nephew. I tried to recover and get the conversation back to my advantage.

'But God sees everything that you're doing Brandon.'

I had to laugh at that one.

You're so right Auntie, God sees the girls and grown women throwing themselves at me every day, at every game and anywhere that I go. He sees my mother having sex outside of marriage, he sees the father that I never knew, doing God knows what, never giving a second thought to the son that he had and neglected to raise. God sees all of this, and nothing has ever prevented me from enjoying and doing whatever I choose to.

'So, all of the years that you've spent with me in my house obeying all of my rules, does that just go out of the window whenever you're out of my sight?'

I wouldn't say that Auntie. You matter to me, and I respect you, so I do what you say and what you expect of me in your presence. Achievement is clearly important to you because you are a doctor, so I do my best at school and on the basketball court even though that's not difficult for me to do at all. Things like that come naturally to me and you know that I thank God for those abilities. I don't run with the wrong crowd because I'm always with Mikasa. I don't drink, or smoke and I don't take advantage of girls or women even though most of the guys on my team do and have slept with practically every girl in the school and any other girls that they can get their hands on. You know that I'm a good man who never gives you any problems. So, my question to you is how do you expect me to be perfect like you if you're not my mother? I mean, this one easy girl that I'm sleeping with; the first one too, I might add, is an issue for you? Did you really expect me to be a virgin until I got married, Aunt Patti?

I had to think before I answered him. I didn't spend any time discussing his body and my expectations for it with him so how could I hold him to a standard now that I never asked him to live by? I didn't get any help from Darius raising him, so I didn't realize that I had failed to teach him some things that were mandatory with Mikasa. I expected him to do something that he was never trained to do and as a woman I wasn't even sure if it was really something that he could do.

I knew that when Darius and I were dating his hormones were always raging and Brandon did not know it, but we didn't abide by the law of God either when it came to saving it for marriage. So how could I judge him now? I looked at my nephew long and hard before I spoke.

'First of all, I'm not perfect son, but didn't I do for you and give you everything that I gave Mikasa?'

I thought that you did Auntie.

'You are such an intelligent, gifted young man and I'm not here to make you feel bad about something that I never taught you, but I will ask you to think about the choices that you're making when it comes to girls, relationships, and intimacy. I don't think that it's fair that women value and save what should be considered so special for men who won't or can't do the same. I just want you to think about it okay?'

I can do that Auntie but if you push me away from Mikasa only God knows what I may get myself into.

'Don't play with me Brandon and don't try to use Mikasa as an excuse. You know right from wrong, and you will begin to develop relationships with other people your age besides Mikasa, do you hear me?

He responded with a feeble yes and I smiled feeling some of the pressure leave my neck. This wasn't the conversation that I expected to have with my nephew today. I paid the bill and hugged him as we left the restaurant.

So, this boy with Mikasa, when do I get to meet him?

Aunt Patti smacked me in the back of my head and sighed as if the conversation that we just had concerning Mikasa had went right over my head.

## DARIUS (the father)

I would walk away from my wife for good if I didn't love her so much. How can I keep Pooch from Mikasa if Patti has already given the boy her stamp of approval?

He was right on my heels coming out of the house and he didn't seem a bit discouraged by any of my questions or my attitude towards him. And my wife just had to bring up our age when we got together. I thought for a moment about how I pursued Patti years ago and how I also recognized that same look of determination in Pooch's' eyes that I had so many years ago. And here goes Patti, trying to compare them with what we had. I don't like it. This boy feels too much too soon, and it is too familiar to me.

We walked down the block and I said, 'I have a few stops to make Pooch so you can shadow me. I will warn you now that it's going to take a lot for you to convince me that you deserve to date my daughter. My standards are high for Mikasa. She is genius material; she is focused, mature and exceptionally beautiful and I know that's what has your attention, but she has a lot more to offer at her age than a lot of grown women do including girls your own age. You don't know how much I would love to keep you away from her but if she wants to date you, I refuse to lose her over you. So now I will be your new best friend. There was silence for a moment and then Pooch spoke.

'I respect you and what you are doing here with me right now. I know that a woman of value is worth protecting, I know that it sets her apart from the rest and that's why Mikasa carries herself the way that she does. She knows her worth, and I also know mine, so I welcome this process. I want you to see for yourself that I am good enough for your daughter and that I have nothing to hide.'

Everything that he said sounded good and appropriate, but time would reveal his true character. We drove in silence as I made my rounds and then we sat outside of my house talking for hours. I got to know a little bit about him, took down his address, his phone number, and his license plate number so that I was satisfied enough to let him take Mikasa out for a few hours. After a short silent pause, I told him, 'You can take Mikasa out tonight but have her home by eleven. It is 6pm now so that will give you ample time to spend talking with her, not kissing, or touching her.

Pooch didn't respond but I heard him take a deep breath as he got out of my car, closed the door, and said, 'Thank you Mr. Jones, I will have her home at eleven and I will see you tomorrow.'

I nodded and said, 'Just call me first and we will take it from there.

## MIKASA

I was in my room reading when I received a text from Pooch letting me know that he would be at my house in fifteen minutes to pick me up.

How did he do it? I can't believe that Daddy is letting me… I had to calm down. I was lying on my bed in my towel after taking a shower that was so refreshing but now, I had to find something to wear quickly. I walked deep into my closet and picked out my sandals first. Mom bought eight pairs of sandals for me for my birthday and the white leather studded pair beckoned me. I picked another colorful silk Pucci halter and white shorts. I checked my hair, glossed my lips, and answered the doorbell.

When I opened the door Pooch's smile warmed me from my toes on up to my eyebrows and inside. I sighed.

'Hello Mikasa, you look so good.'

I smiled and he said, 'You smell just like a sugar cookie, what is that? I could eat you girl.'

Don't tease me. I missed you.

There was an awkward silence.

'I missed you too. We have a reservation at this fondue place; are you ready?'

We headed towards the door, and he kissed me on the lips much to my surprise.

'I had to get that in before we got outside. I have to put your father at ease with me seeing you. I don't know how you feel about that or how you really feel about me, but I like you Mikasa. I…… lets go. We can talk about it in the restaurant. Did I tell you how good you look?'

I laughed and we left the house and drove to the restaurant. Dru Hill was playing all the way there. Neither of us said a word during the drive but as soon as we parked, I kissed Pooch and said, 'You know how I feel; I like you too. You held your own with my father this morning and that's not easy to do. You're not intimidated by him, and I'm impressed by that.

Pooch sat back a minute absorbing it all as I opened my door. He noticed, quickly exited, grabbed my hand, and closed my door just to reopen it for me. We entered the restaurant and were led to our table. Moments later the waiter began to set up and bring dishes to our table.

Pooch said, 'I took the liberty of calling ahead to order. I figured that I would beat you to it this time.'

A server appeared with a plate of hot towels, and I smiled as she set it down and I said, 'Give me your hands.'

Pooch lifted his hands up together and I wrapped a towel around them. I held them there for a moment and then I cleaned each of his hands individually taking my time around each nail. Pooch did the same for me and we watched each other for a moment before he began to feed me from the fondue in the center of the table.

How many girls have you done this for?

'Done what?'

How many girls have you hand fed on the first date?

'How many guys hands have you cleaned like that?'

I smiled.

I have only sort of done that for my father once. My mother always went through the hand cleansing ritual for my father at home before we ate each meal. I thought that it looked fun to do but when I attempted to clean my dad's hands on one occasion, he didn't hesitate to let me know that it was Mommy's job, so I was upset of course. Now that I've done it for you, and I'm older, I understand why it is my mothers' job. Sometimes the simplest gesture can be so intimate. It can feel like a kiss or a caress. Sometimes it's all about how you feel when you do something. I guess whenever we touch, I feel something like how I feel right now when you fed me. It's something I haven't felt before.

So, what about you, how many women have you fed?

'I never fed anyone but myself Mikasa. It just feels right with you.'

He continued to feed me and himself. I tried to feed him too, but he resisted. When the fruit and chocolate fondue came out, he let me feed him slowly and now I resisted him feeding me. We sat in the restaurant for hours enjoying each other's company. When we left the restaurant and got in the car, I asked him to go to the game room on Main Street and he agreed. We rode along in silence for a while and then he asked, 'When exactly do you leave for school and where is it again?'

Classes at Vassar begin in the last week of August and the school is in Poughkeepsie. If we're still together next month, you can come there with me one afternoon. I will be staying in the dorm. Why do you ask?

"Well, I would like to plan our summer together. I 'm also concerned about the distance keeping us apart, but an hour isn't far at all and why would you say if we're together? You know that I'll be here next month and the month after that and next year. Don't you feel this between us? I mean, I know it's only day two, but I'm claiming you as mine already, so really, the distance to your college, or any distance for that matter will keep us apart."

Well, just tell me how you really feel. You seem so sure of yourself, but we just met. How can you say with such confidence that we will really vibe like that? I mean, what I feel is intense but…actually, don't answer, let's change the subject because I feel the same way, to be honest.

Pooch asked, "So, are you excited about Vassar?"

I'm excited, nervous and a little scared about being away from my parents. I 've never been away from them, not even for summer camp, so it will be different. My mother is excited because she always wanted to go away to college. My Dad, well you see how he is. He is suspicious of everyone with me, the professors, the students, he always thinks someone is up to something. I think that he plans to interview every man on campus, and it's just embarrassing. I mean he acts as if men are lurking everywhere just waiting to pounce on me.

The other issue with him is that he acts as if I won't need him anymore, but I love my dad so much that I thought he was secure in that. I don't know how to convince him that I will always need and love him.

Pooch paused and said, 'It can't be easy for him. You are his only child. My Mom was always protective of me although she did her best to hide it. Once you're away it will be important for you to keep in constant contact with him to let him know how you are. Sometimes we feel a certain way about the people who are closest to us, but we don't convey it enough. Try to make it your business to remind him that he's important. Personally, I can't imagine how it feels to have a daughter, but I understand that it's a special relationship. I see how your dad treats you and I hope to have a daughter one day. I would love to have a mini Mikasa.'

## BRANDON

It's Sunday, a day I usually spend with my two favorite people, Mikasa and Aunt Patti. So, you can only imagine my surprise when we get to church, and Uncle Darius and company are present dressed in two of the nicest suits I've ever seen, and both are smiling from ear to ear. Simultaneously Aunt Patti and Mikasa do double takes since Uncle Darius hasn't been to church in a month of Sundays. The guy with him had two separately wrapped lilies in his hand and my heart sank as he moved toward us and handed one to Mikasa and one to my aunt. They both smiled at him and Mikasa's skin was glowing. Mikasa turned to me and said, 'Brandon this is Darius, Darius this is Brandon.' Without thinking but suddenly remembering where I'd seen him before, I gave him a dap and said what's up as heat traveled up my neck. I moved towards my uncle to greet him and suddenly I felt out of place. The new guy who I recognized from Jada's block grabbed Mikasa's' hand in his and Uncle Darius did the same with Aunt Patti. We moved to the pew and sat down with me in the middle of Aunt Patti and Mikasa. I felt Uncle Darius watching me as I watched the new guy. I felt the usual attention naturally bestowed upon Mikasa and Aunt Patti at every service, but the energy was different today. The choir sang, the Pastor preached, the benediction went forth and all the while Mikasa's hand remained in his.

As we prepared to exit the church the Pastor made his way toward us and greeted us. "Sister Patti, how are you and who do you have here?"

'Hello, Pastor, I've never been better. My family is here, and that Word was for me, praise God! This is……

Uncle Darius interrupted.

"I'm Darius Jones, Sister Patti's husband."

Pooch stepped forward next.

'I am Darius Jackson, Mikasa's friend.'

"Sister Patti, my, my, have you been keeping your husband a secret all this time?" He turned to shake my uncles' hand, but he didn't look him in the eye.

He continued.

"And you know my son will sure be disappointed that he couldn't speak to your daughter today. She's such a beautiful girl.

He said this as he shook the new guys' hand while also avoiding looking him directly in the eye. "You have a nice family here." He stood for a moment as if he were waiting for one of us to respond.

'Oh yes, thank you Pastor.'

"You're welcome, Sister Patti. Have a blessed day now; all of you."

Aunt Patti was startled a bit as we moved out the door. Uncle Darius wanted to say something but didn't.

How should my aunt respond to the Pastor saying that she was keeping my uncle a secret? Secret: what was the secret? Had he asked her status before?

New guy responded to the Pastors' parting words not missing a beat. 'You do the same, see you next week.'

Uncle Darius glared at the Pastor and briefly glanced at Pooch.

Pooch sensed my uncles' anger and said, 'It looks like these ladies will need our company here every week. I hope you don't mind if I join you, Mr. Jones? I don't know how I feel about Pastor Johnson right now, but that Word sure spoke to me. I've missed this since I lost my family. Thank you, Mr. Jones, for letting me join you at this service with you and the family today.'

Uncle Darius was still thrown off by the Pastor's remark but recovered quickly and said, 'Even though I never cared much for that Pastor I agree that attending service seems necessary now for more reasons than one. I plan to set my feelings aside, seek God and enjoy the time with my family also. So that sounds like a plan Darius.'

Aunt Patti was pleasantly surprised by her husband's response, but I was getting pissed. Sundays were always my time alone with my two favorite people. I had them all to myself for so long and now not only did I have to stay away from Mikasa during the week now I can't be next to her exclusively on Sundays either. What in the world is going on?

I had gotten so accustomed to having them both to myself that I really don't know how to feel right now. Uncle Darius watched me watch every move Pooch made while I also stole glances at Mikasa, but she wasn't paying me any mind of course because her friend was there. Everyone was happy now except for me.

## Chapter 6 – WHAT DOES DARIUS KNOW?

Listen, let's go to brunch, my treat. I know that you and Mikasa have plans Pooch, but I would like to spend a little time with you two today and I know that we all could use a bite to eat.

Everyone agreed as we began to walk to the parking lot. Brandon was following Mikasa, and I said, 'Brandon come and ride with us.'

I turned towards my aunt and uncle, and I was steaming inside as I got in the back seat of their car.

At the restaurant before my wife could say a word Brandon slid in the booth beside Mikasa. Pooch was already seated on the other side of her. Pooch glanced at Brandon briefly as Patti was looking his way, but he acted as if he was totally engrossed in the menu.

He's testing my patience.

The server brought the water to the table and Brandon picked up Mikasa's' napkin, unraveled her utensils and then he did his own. He then picked up the juice pitcher and proceeded to pour juice for everyone except Pooch. I frowned at him.

As soon as the server walked off, I said, "So Brandon, how are you?

He looked at me. It had been a long time since he sat under my spotlight, and I could see that it was long overdue.

"I'm good Uncle D."

How is school?

"Easy. You know that Mikasa and I never have a problem with getting good grades." He smiled at Mikasa, and she smiled back.

What about practice? It seems as if you are in the paper every week. Does anyone else on the team get any love?

"Well, you know that my skills are impeccable, and I continue to score the most points at every game that Mikasa attends but you have not been to one of my games in months. I would love to see all my family at all my games. As you know my mother rarely bothers to attend. She's always working."

'Well, you realize that you have my support even when I'm not there. You have so much talent and I'm immensely proud of you.'

I looked across the table at my uncle. He never complimented me in the past and now I was totally caught off guard.

Do you mean that?

'Mean what Brandon?'

You're proud of me, really? I didn't even think that you liked me. It seems like I'm always on your last nerve.

Mikasa and Patti were startled by his comment as Pooch silently sat and observed.

'You're my nephew, what are you saying? I care about everybody and everything that Patti cares about. But you know what, this is a conversation for another time. Let's discuss it further after your next game, okay?'

I wanted him to continue to compliment me, but I nodded at my uncle in agreement. My uncle turned his focus on Pooch and said, 'Darius, tell us about your family. Where are they from?'

"Well, my grandparents live in Greenville, North Carolina but I haven't been back there since my parents passed away."

Patti and I apologized again for his loss and Mikasa touched his hand lightly. He continued to speak. "I was so angry for so long about losing my parents. I hated God for taking them away from me. But then I met your daughter, or should I say saw her for the first time and I started to feel something other than anger for a change. Something about Mikasa, just watching her, started to help me to feel normal again, my anger has greatly diminished since I first saw her and that was comforting to me. My grandparents were on my mind all the time and I think I'm ready to see them and the rest of the family now because I do miss them.

Mikasa tells me that you also have family in North Carolina."

I looked at Mikasa and she was grinning slyly at him. The server returned with the food, I blessed it, and we all began to eat. After eating half of my food, I rested my fork down and said, 'My parents are from Raleigh, and we will just leave it at that for now.' Pooch smiled and glanced at Mikasa.

When everyone was done eating Patti said, "Darius I'm glad that you joined us today and I appreciate your honesty about your feelings about God. Things happen in life that we never expect, and it's good that you're finding your way back to Him. You seem like a genuinely nice young man, and I'm praying that you don't disappoint me."

'Thank you, Mrs. Jones, and believe me I won't. I really like Mikasa. Just ask her to be gentle with me.' He smiled at Patti. I was stone faced during their exchange and so was Brandon.

I looked at Mikasa then at Brandon's' frowning face and noticed that it was becoming increasingly difficult for the boy to hide his feelings for Mikasa and if Patti didn't see it now, she's just in denial. I paid the bill, and we exited the restaurant. Mikasa and Pooch said their goodbyes to us and began to walk to the car.

Brandon said, 'Where are you two going? Can I come?'

Patti and I both said no in unison and Patti said,

'Did you forget that we have a date, Brandon? You and I have things to finish from yesterday.'

I frowned at Patti knowing that words like that made him feel like he was her man instead of her nephew. She hugged me and led Brandon towards her car.

He sighed not wanting to continue the conversation that he had with his aunt yesterday. When they got back to the house, he began to question his aunt.

"Isn't Mikasa too young to date? Do you know that he was holding her hand throughout the whole service? Who is he anyway, really?"

'What are you talking about? Do not question me boy. Who are you to decide if Mikasa is ready to date and why were you watching them during service? That isn't what you were there for, and you are acting selfish since you are two years younger, and you're dating already.'

"Well, I don't think that he's right for her. I'm just saying."

'Is that right? You're just saying? I don't think that Kim is right for you, being seventeen and all, but you made your choice, didn't you? Mikasa's life and who she dates is her father and my business not yours so stay in your place. We were having such a wonderful day together; why are you trying to spoil it now? You know what…let's change the subject. Are you excited about prom?'

I wanted to continue to debate with my aunt about Mikasa dating but I knew that I was working her nerves, so I pulled back for now. "Speaking of prom, I am still a little nervous about dancing. I am clumsy sometimes, so I really need Mikasa to practice with me one last time right before the prom, okay? I really want to impress Kim."

'You want to impress who?'

Come on Auntie, you just said her name, Kim.

Now I was suspicious. You don't spend any time with Kim, she's so fast by your description of her but now you want to impress her with your dance moves?'

Well, I just want to show off at the prom, but I didn't think that you wanted to hear that. It sounds selfish.

I was apprehensive about Brandon and everything to do with his prom, but I said okay and suddenly after agreeing to his request my normal nephew returned and we laughed and joked our way through the rest of the afternoon.

After all the projects we started together were complete I cooked, and we sat at the dining table to eat. We finished eating and after a while Brandon became restless and asked, 'So when is Mikasa coming home?'

## MIKASA

We arrived at the pier to a 100-foot yacht. As we approached the entrance of the yacht, we were met by a brown-skinned guy that looked to be in his twenties. Pooch introduced him to me as Skip, a childhood friend. Skip looked at me for what seemed to be the longest moment ever then said, 'How nice to meet you Mikasa; welcome aboard.'

As I got on the boat I was surprised once again that my father agreed to this outing. I couldn't imagine what Pooch did or said to convince him, but he seemed to be endearing himself to my father rather quickly.

We sat inside and Skip made light conversation with us, but he couldn't seem to help staring at me. I figured that he wanted to continue to talk so I said, 'So, tell me something interesting about Pooch that you think that no one else knows about?'

Skip smiled and thought about it for a moment, but Pooch was frowning. We sat in silence for a bit then Skip said, 'Well he acts really tough, but he is a sucker for a pretty lady.'

Pooch tensed up.

Oh really? So how many pretty ladies has he brought on this boat? I was smiling trying to tease more information out of Skip, but Pooch clearly was not pleased, and it was his turn to speak.

"We just got on this boat Skip, and you're stirring it up already? Why would you say something like that? Since when, have I, been a sucker for any woman Skip?"

He tried to look around as if he were innocent, but I could tell that he was the type of 'friend' that enjoyed pushing Pooch's buttons. I sat beside Pooch and stroked his thigh, but he was agitated. I said, "Don't be mad baby. I know that he is playing; just trying to get you worked up. Why don't we step out by the front of the boat and enjoy the weather? Is anyone else on the boat with us?"

Skip replied, 'No it's just the three of us. I invited a lady friend but she's not here yet so we can shove off if you're ready. He addressed me directly.

Would you like a Mimosa Mikasa?'

"She doesn't drink Skip, but we would both like half and half, orange juice and cranberry juice please. Could you get that for us yourself and give us a moment?"

Skip looked insulted but he walked towards the bar as we stepped out. Pooch spoke with haste, "Listen, Mikasa, I wanted to do something special for you today, something out of the ordinary but my friend is really acting out of character. This doesn't seem to be a good idea. I don't know what is up with him so let me apologize in advance for his behavior. And in reference to the statements that he made, and I don't mean to sound cocky but please understand that I never have to work for the attention of a woman and my experience with you and what I'm willing to do to be with you is a first for me."

I was impressed with his response, but I felt it was unnecessary.

Pooch, you don't have to explain anything to me. I know that you had a life before you met me. You don't have to justify anything to me about your past. He seems to be having a good time with this and I'm not in the least bit offended so just relax and let's see how far he goes with it. I have no reason to believe anything that he says considering your reaction so let it flow. I'm cool if you are cool so, why pass up a nice boat ride?

My reaction to his friends' antics seemed to calm Pooch and as Skip approached with the drinks, he seemed more at ease.

"So, Mikasa, where did you meet my boy?"

Pooch sipped his juice with a stoic look on his face. I thought for a moment about my response and said, 'I'm not proud of it, but we met after my shift at the strip club. He was so focused on my moves, and he threw so many hundreds at me during my routine that I figured he deserved to meet me personally. It was surreal because he looked past my red lipstick and practically naked body and saw and respected the real me and we've been inseparable ever since.

Pooch looked at me in shock and then doubled over in laughter. Skip was so enthralled with me that it took him a minute to catch on that I was indeed telling him a story.

Pooch couldn't stop laughing so Skip frowned and finally said, 'Okay Pooch so maybe when you catch your breath you can tell me how it really went down. I mean, I would love to meet a woman like you Mikasa, but I need to know where to look. Do you have any sisters?'

I don't have any sisters, but I'm curious about something that you just said. What type of woman do you think I am?

This made Pooch pause and he said, 'Skip, be careful about how you answer. I don't want to knock you out on your own boat. We have been friends for years and I never saw this side of you before. Remember that we are boys.'

'Yes, we are boys, but I'm intrigued with your date and to answer your question Mikasa you're beautiful, interesting and you seem to be a bit crafty.'

Well thank you for the compliments. I can accept that, but I have a few questions for you. What is a friend and what type of friend are you? You agreed with my man that you've been friends for years so break that down for me please.

Skip acted as if he couldn't hear clearly. He coughed to clear his throat and feigned ignorance.

'Excuse me, what was the question?'

Okay, I can repeat it if you are willing to answer but if you aren't, feel free to say so.

With that Pooch responded.

"You don't have to answer Skip and you don't have to ask my girl any more questions either.

I really wish Teneka were here with you because now we are lopsided. I planned this outing with you for us to be coupled up, so I could spend some quality time with Mikasa. I thought you had a similar plan in mind with your girl. I didn't bring Mikasa here for you to interrogate her. So, if it's all right with you just give us some space and you can drop us back at the dock and get on with your night."

'That's fine Pooch, I understand, but may I answer her question?'

"Oh, you want to answer now? Go ahead."

'A friend is what I am to him Mikasa. A friend cares about who his friends associate with, and cares about that friend getting hurt. A friend has your back and is down for whatever with you. He had a wicked smile on his face as he continued. A friend expects that friend to also have someone for him of like quality and a friend knows when to back off, he said and left the room.'

He walked off as we looked at each other in amazement.

## POOCH

### What was that?

I can't believe that Skip was trying to clown me after all these years and of all times in front of Mikasa. I wanted to deal with his case immediately, but I couldn't resist doing what I had been thinking about ever since we stepped on the boat, so I kissed Mikasa like I was waiting to kiss her all day. It felt so good to finally be alone with her and it felt even better to have her in my arms. I couldn't believe how familiar and comfortable her rhythm and warmth felt to me and man, why did her kiss feel so good?

Mikasa paused, stopping me. 'You're too much, what are you doing to me?' She said this and held her chest.

What am I doing to you?

'Yes, what are you doing to me? I've never felt how I felt when I kissed you and you had the nerve to tell my mother earlier that I need to be careful with you! You need to be careful with me. I shouldn't feel like this so soon. I mean, I don't have anything to compare it to really, since I've never been kissed by anyone except family but just stop making it feel so good Pooch.'

I smiled at her, put my lips back on hers and it was on again. It felt as if sparks were shooting throughout my legs, straight up my spine and I never wanted to stop kissing her. I backed her against the wall and then I stopped myself. I was getting too excited too fast, and her fathers' voice replayed in my mind. We sat down, I leaned my head back to slow my pulse down as I held her hand in mine. I spoke softly near her ear.

Tell me, why does it feel like I have always known you Mikasa? You're so special.

'And so are you, Pooch. I can't believe that it took so long for us to get together. I mean, way that I'm feeling now, I'm glad that Brandon kept the other guys away from me but you; imagine if we got together a year ago?' We sat and thought for a minute but all that came to mind for me was the fact that Mikasa would've been fifteen with me eighteen and that would have felt impossible at that time.

You know I did imagine it and usually I'm all for getting what I want as soon as I can, but I believe that watching you for so long only increased my desire for you. I feel like I learned a lot about you by watching you and I think that the delay made me more appealing to you also. And if you think that your father is having a tough time letting you date now, just imagine you at fifteen. It really would have been a struggle to convince him that I was not a perv. That year made me realize that I had to have you and that I was determined to have you no matter how long it took. The magnetism between us; the attraction that we share I know that your parents feel it and I also know that may sound too deep, but the way that your mother reacted and the way that your father reacted just seemed like they knew. Your mother seems as if she accepts it but your dad, of course, would like to push me as far away from you as possible because he knows what it means and exactly what it could lead to.

Mikasa looked as if she wanted to speak. It seemed as if many thoughts were passing through her mind, but we just sat in silence holding each other's hand. The silence was comfortable, and she began to rub my thigh.

I began to kiss her again and immediately felt warm. When I finally came up for air, I opened my eyes and Skip was standing right outside the doorway watching us. Mikasa was facing me and couldn't see him. After a few moments I excused myself and went out to see what was up. When I approached Skip the first thing out of his mouth was, 'Honey is fine! Where have you been hiding here?'

I know that she's fine, and I haven't been hiding her; this is our second date Skip and here we are on your boat. I thought that it would be nice and peaceful for me to finally get here, but what's up with you? Why are you acting like you never saw me with a girl before?

'Second date, isn't this the girl you told me about last year?'

Did you just hear what I said to you?

'Yes, I heard you I heard you. She's so different from the other girls I 've seen you with. She has some spunk and is so pretty. I have to admit that I'm intrigued but I meant no disrespect. So, is she the girl man?'

Yes, Mikasa is that girl. We were with her parents this morning. Prior to the last few days her cousin was around her all this time blocking but she finally came around without him and I seized the opportunity.

'Wait a minute, back up, her parents; you were with her parents? Doesn't she go to Hunter with you? Why were you with her parents already?'

You're asking too many questions, and you're all up in my business. Is everything cool with you? You're really acting strange.

'I'm good man. You just surprised me with her. I couldn't help but ask. I'll behave. Does she have a sister?'

I scowled at him. Didn't you ask that already? No, she doesn't have a sister.

'What about her mom?'

Just stop. Her mother is fine too but she's married to Mikasa's father. I'm going back to Mikasa. You need to get your mind right. We will talk another time. Skip tried to protest but I was done.

I returned to find Mikasa comfortably seated on the side of the boat enjoying the view. As I got closer to her, she turned and stood up.

I apologize for leaving you alone like that. I wanted to see what was up with Skip. Why don't you come over here so that I can show you some of my favorite spots out here on the water?

I walked over to Pooch, and we stood for an hour looking out at the water and talking. His voice and the movement of the water were so relaxing.

"I have some questions to ask you Pooch."

Okay.

"Do you have a girlfriend?"

He laughed while holding me in his arms with his nose in my hair. He released me slowly, looked me in the eyes and said, 'Of course not Mikasa. Do you think that I would have asked your parents to date you if I had a girlfriend? Do you think that I'm crazy?

"Well, I didn't think to ask you when I met you and my dad schooled me about getting mad with someone about something that I never asked. I feel like you are an honest man, but I had to ask. My father asked me all these questions about you the other night and I couldn't answer any of them because all the questions that I asked you in the restaurant focused on your character. I couldn't tell him anything besides your age which he thought he knew already.

My other question is, are you serious about coming to church again? You surprised me this morning when you showed up with my dad."

Oh, I'm very serious about that, Mikasa. I was raised in church. We attended service and bible study every week. My relationship with God was particularly important to me until I lost both of my parents.

Your Dad, well his way of allowing us to date is kind of cool because it helps me recognize what I had with my father, and I really miss him so interacting with your dad isn't bad at all. I felt so alone for a while and now I'm starting to feel like I belong somewhere thanks to you and your family. It's amazing how comfortable I feel with you. So far, I've told you more in two days than I've ever told any other girl in my life besides my mother so if you want to know anything feel free to ask. I think that if we're honest with each other, we should never have any problems.

Now I have a question for you. Do you have a boyfriend? I don't see how it would be possible the way your cousin has been blocking but I have to ask.

"No, I don't have a boyfriend and I really wasn't interested in one until now. I was so content with life that I didn't even realize that I was missing all of this. I motioned up and down at him and he smiled.

I'm happy that you are so comfortable with me and my family and please don't take my cousins' behavior or attitude towards you personally. He treats anyone who comes close to me the same way. We have been each other's everything for so long that he doesn't want to let go, grow up and move on. We were raised together like siblings but conveniently he tends to forget that I am the oldest. He also forgets that he's not my father and as you saw today my father resents that behavior in him. My father is so protective of the relationship that he and I have, and he doesn't like the fact that Brandon tries to come between us."

I can't blame your dad at all. I don't want anybody coming too close to you either and that includes your cousin.

Suddenly Skip appeared again.

"Dinner is served. Are you two ready to eat?"

I looked at my man. I asked him earlier to take us back to the dock, but he seemed to be ignoring everything that I said to him tonight.

Skip, I thought that I asked you to take us back to the dock.

"We are headed back but what type of host would I be if I didn't offer you and your lady something to eat?"

I looked at Mikasa then back at him. Alright Skip, we're right behind you.

"It's just me and the captain, so we have light fare. Deli sandwiches, salads, shrimp cocktail, Triple Chocolate Layer cake and Trifle."

Sounds good to me, how gracious of you Skip, Mikasa said.

Pooch took my hand and led me inside to the table. On the right side of the table there was a dish of water and pristine white towels. We sat around the table in the center of the room and Pooch soaked one towel in the steaming water and wiped my hands. He dried them then washed his own since he was closer to the dish, but then he handed me the towel to dry his hands. Of course, I loved the attention, but Skips' eyes were glued to us, watching it all. I waited for both guys to prepare the plates and then Pooch blessed the food. Skip was still absorbed in what just occurred.

We began to eat and then Skip spoke.

"So, Mikasa, where did you really meet Pooch?"

Mikasa bit her sandwich, smiled, and said, 'I met Pooch over a year ago on Fordham Road.

"Really? He's so lucky that he met you first. You're a good-looking girl. How old are you?"

I gave him a look that said I will kill you if you ask her another question. I looked at her and said, 'You don't have to answer. He should know better than to ask a woman her age.'

"Okay I apologize for that one."

I glared at him again.

'Why don't you let Mikasa eat and then we can play twenty questions later okay?'

We ate in silence as Skip brazenly kept his eyes on Mikasa. My temperature was rising again but I played it cool. I pondered Skips' questions wondering why he was purposely trying to aggravate me.

Mikasa ate about a third of what was on her plate, took a sip of her drink and pushed her plate away. Skip got up to get the dessert and I pushed my plate back too, fed up with his behavior. We finally docked so I took another towel, wiped Mikasa hands and mine while we stood up.

Listen man we're going to head out. Thanks for everything.

"What, no dessert?

Nah, man but thanks. Skip extended his hand to Mikasa and when she shook it, he pulled her towards him to hug her. She was a bit stunned but said, "Thank you so much, goodnight, Skip."

"My pleasure Mikasa, please come again."

We stepped off the boat and walked to the car. When I turned the key in the ignition Dru Hill was softly playing and I was silent.

'What's wrong babe?'

Nothing.

'Despite your friend's behavior I had a nice time with you so don't let him upset you.'

I smiled and caressed her hand.

Why are you watching me Mikasa, I'm fine. I was smiling now, and frowning because I didn't want the day to end.

'I like looking at you. I can't help myself.'

You can't help yourself Mikasa? Why do you like looking at me? What do you see when you look at me?

'I see a handsome, intelligent brother with a lot going for himself. I see a man with excellent taste in women and in cars. I see a sensitive man who has intense emotions. I see....

Okay Mikasa, I don't mean to interrupt, but can I tell you what I see?

'Well of course you can.'

I see my absolutely, beautiful, divine match sitting beside me where she must always be.

'I didn't hear you well. What do you see?'

I smiled and reveled in the fact that just talking to Mikasa calmed me tremendously and I was no longer angry about Skip. 'I said that I see my absolutely beautiful, divine match sitting beside me where she must always be.'

'Wow, I like that, Darius. I've never been described in such a magnificent way. Do you really feel that way about me?'

I do.

'So does that mean that we are dating exclusively?'

Yes, it does.

I sat back in my seat and thought about us. I thought about going to school all week and missing Pooch and ....

Are you all right with us dating exclusively Mikasa?

'Yes, of course I am. I just hope that I can keep up with you and that you will be patient with me.'

What do you mean keep up with me and don't you see that I'm patient?

'I'm only sixteen so I guess I'm concerned about the girls in your classes, girls that probably are throwing themselves at you all of the time.'

I smiled and said, "Don't worry about that Mikasa. I've been focused on you for over a year. Now that we're seeing each other nothing is farther from my mind than other girls. As far as I'm concerned, there aren't any other girls, and your age is irrelevant. You're so beautiful and different that I can't imagine ever losing interest in you. And now that you are voicing your concerns, I will voice mine.

I have issues with the boys in your school and men in general stepping out of line with you. Tonight, my own friend couldn't keep his eyes off you so whatever you are feeling trust that I feel it too.

'Well, I guess that we just have to see how all of this plays out.'

You don't have to worry about me Mikasa, I'm yours.

'And I'm yours but what's up with the music. Did my dad tell you that I like Dru Hill?

This made Pooch smile. 'No, he didn't. I can't even picture your father telling me about anything that you like, anytime soon. This music is just something that we have in common. "Beauty" is my anthem and since I met you, I've played it every day and "These are the Times" is a close second. My parents used to listen to Dru Hill all the time so I guess it was inevitable that I would like their sound. They say a lot of the things that are in my heart.

'Mine too and those are my mothers and now my two favorite songs. I play them all the time too.

We stopped at the mall to get Mrs. Fields chocolate chip cookies and Pooch kissed me before he got out. He left the car on as I sat back while he went to get the cookies. When he got back to the car he was smiling.

I hope you like milk chocolate chips; I forgot to ask you, forgive me for being rude. I went to call you and noticed that I'd left the phone in the car with you. I bought three big cookies for you and three for me, and a dozen nibblers for your mom.

I smiled back at him just as bright. 'I love milk chocolate, thank you and I'm so glad that you are smiling again.'

I headed for Mikasa's house and got to her home in twenty minutes flat. It was five minutes to eleven when she stepped into her house after kissing me goodnight.

## BRANDON

Decisions, decisions which one should I get? The princess cut, or brilliant cut diamond tennis bracelet. I think that her studs are princess cut. I signaled the salesperson.

Excuse me, how much is this bracelet? The man sauntered over slowly assuming that I was a window shopper. I sensed his attitude but persisted with my questions. 'May I see that tennis bracelet right there?'

He unlocked the case and took the bracelet bar out.

How many carats is that? What's the clarity, and how much is it?

'This bracelet is four carats, H class, VVS. The price is $11,000.'

I pulled out my wallet removing the debit card my mom gave me years ago. There was a substantial balance available on my card, so I continued to shop. "May I also see the necklace over there that goes with this bracelet?

Now the man's' brows were raised, he was smiling and finally moving like he had some sense.

'One moment sir, I'll be right back with that.'

"So now I'm sir?" I said to myself. Salespeople are so funny. People in general are funny.

He returned with two necklaces, one six carat and one eight carats. Of course, I chose the eight carats. I held the bracelet and necklace in my hand admiring the clarity of the stones.

She will like this. How much is the necklace?

'$18,000, eight carats, also H class VVS. I also have earrings for $1300, same class and clarity. Is this for your mother young man?'

"No, these are for my girl, and she has earrings already, but you can show me one four carat stud and I will give you $25,000 for everything."

The salesperson wasted no time grabbing my card, the earring, necklace, and bracelet. He polished, boxed, and bagged everything up, and handed me the receipt. He pressed a business card in my hand and asked, 'What team do you play for?'

I laughed, "Seneca Valley High School but I'm headed to the pros."

The man was surprised but said, "Well whenever you need jewelry don't hesitate to call or come see me again. You are guaranteed the best stones at the best prices. He shook my hand, and I left the store.

Next stop was the tailor at Saks. Ever since I turned eleven, Ma began taking me to 5th Avenue to acclimate me with wearing fine tailored suits. She always said that you get what you pay for and if you pay enough, you can have anything that you want. I thought about that for a moment and now that I was older it rang true. The taller that I grew the more it cost me, but I always found a suit at Saks that flattered my frame. Today I decided to pick up two suits, a grey one and a white one. Everyone always commented on my style, so I had to do it up, and for Mikasa I had to look my best. She didn't know it yet, but she was in for some real surprises.

She doesn't know that she's going with me to the prom; she doesn't know that I bought her a Vera Wang classic and the jewels and shoes will really push it over the top. It would be nice if she wore her hair up but any way that she wears it I know that it will look good. In fact, let me call her beauty salon and nail salon now to make appointments and pay for the services. I will conveniently call Kim on Friday morning with my sick excuse to get her out of the way.

I have my shoes, three shirts, two ties, silk boxers and undershirts, two kerchiefs and two pairs of diamond cufflinks. My personal shopper Chanel always takes care of me, and I know that she is dying for me to hit that, but I know what I want, and she's not it. I would also like to get that French perfume for Mikasa that she always wears but I better quit while I am ahead since her dad always gets it. I'm at about seventeen grand right now including the Maybach lease and I hope that Mikasa will agree to the mixed dance session at the W Hotel after the prom. I hate to lie to her but honestly, she was my only choice all along.

Kim only sees dollar signs when she sees me anyway and as her personal sex toy. The second part is mutual for me, but it will never keep me with her. No one loves me like Mikasa.

It's Monday evening, and I must get these things home and tucked away so that I can get over to Mikasa's. It's about 8pm so she should be out of the shower and relaxing when I get there. I pressed the doorbell.

She looked through the peephole and opened the door smiling.

'What's up B?'

Hi Mikasa, I sang. You look cute. Listen, I have a game on Wednesday at the Polo Grounds. Can you and Jada come please?

'Of course, we will be there. Are you coming in?'

No cousin, I have to study and see Kim for a minute. Don't forget that we are practicing on Friday before the prom. Thanks, love you.

He was closing the door before I could even respond.

Back at the house I checked everything I purchased again and then laid down. Before long I was dreaming about Mikasa in the little pink shorts and cutoff sweatshirt she opened the door wearing.

Fast forward, the school week was flying by, and I was warming up for my game on Wednesday. Mikasa, Jada and my Aunt Patti arrived early wearing shorts and pretty silk tee shirts. I played the best game of my life as they cheered, waved, and whistled at every shot I made all throughout the game. My teammates were sweating me at halftime when Mikasa came over and threw her arms around my neck to congratulate me. I lifted her off the floor a little and kissed her cheek, enjoying the attention. I finished the game scoring the most points and rushed to shower and change as the crowd ran up on me, slapping fives and hugging me as we ran into the locker room.

'Who was that B?' I knew that the questions would begin as soon as I got in the locker room. Who?

'Honey that hugged you, and the two girls with her. They are all fine but Shorty, she is the truth!'

That is my family man, "Shorty" is my cousin, and she has a man, my aunt who is her mother is married to my uncle and the other *girl* is my cousins' friend.

'Your aunt? Her mother? Which one? They all look the same age and none of them look like you. Hook a brother up, they are not your family man. Come on.'

I laughed and walked out of the locker room. Mikasa and Aunt Patti hugged me and congratulated me simultaneously. I favored Mikasa's' side of course and touched her hair gently as she held onto me. I looked at Jada and said, 'Come on, I know that you want to hug me too!'

She blushed and rushed over to hug me. I knew that she liked me the moment that she saw me. We left the park and Aunt Patti dropped me off at the house. I got out and thanked them again for coming out. I was floating on a cloud. I ate my dinner alone, watched television and went to bed. I always preferred to eat at Aunt Patti's but tonight I was all right reveling in my moment of victory. As I drifted off to sleep Mikasa's pretty, smiling face and silky hair bounced back and forth in my dreams.

Thursday was a blur. I awoke Friday morning to a still house, my mother was off to work already, and it was only 7AM. I called Kim at once and let her know that I didn't feel well and wouldn't be taking her to the prom.

'I think that I have the flu. I feel awful. You can take someone else, and I will pay for everything.'

She protested saying that she couldn't go without me. I felt bad for a moment then said, 'I don't want you to miss your prom girl, go ahead and find someone.' She continued to refuse. I need to rest now. I will call you tomorrow or when I feel better okay?'

She offered to take care of me, but I refused. I ended the call and dialed Mikasa's number.

Good morning Mikasa, how are you and help me please!

'What's up Brandon?'

Kim is sick and I can't go to prom alone!

'Brandon, I have a date tonight.'

Mikasa please, I only have one prom, you've been helping me so much and I'm so excited about it. Please.

There was silence as she pondered my request.

'What time is your prom?'

Yes!

'I just asked you the time I did not say yes yet. I don't have anything to wear, my hair isn't done, and my nails and toes are a mess.'

Your nails and toes are fine Mikasa. They always are but not to worry I have it all covered. You get out of school today at 12, right?

'Yes.'

Okay I don't have any classes today so I will pick you up from school and get your hair, nails and toes done. I will buy you a dress this morning. This will be completely stress free for you. I swear and tell Pooch that I apologize for breaking your date.

'Let me call Mommy. She's at work already. Goodbye Brandon.

I hung up the phone with the broadest smile ever on my face.

## Chapter 7 – SO STRANGE

What a strange week this has been. I saw Pooch every day except Wednesday, and he was so distracted when I spoke to him. I went to Brandon's game that day, which was fun but here I am on Friday stuck with my cousin again.

'Hello, may I please speak to Dr. Jones?' My mother responded. 'Dr Jones speaking.'

Hi Mom, I'm going to the prom with Brandon tonight.

'Hello Mikasa. Why?'

Kim is sick. She called him this morning.

'Aw baby girl, you know that you don't have to go if you don't want to. Aren't you going out with Pooch tonight?'

Well, yes, but I know how much this means to Brandon. He's so excited about his prom and us practicing his dance moves. I just figured that he would owe me big for this. He's picking me up from school to get my hair, nails and toes done. He is also buying me a dress.

'What! A dress, why?'

I don't know. He must have a fancy suit since he insists on buying me a dress. Do you mind if I see Pooch after the prom for a little while? I don't want to cancel on him completely at the last minute. The prom starts at 7PM so we should be back at midnight.

'That shouldn't be a problem Mikasa but don't be surprised if the prom lasts longer than you think. Doesn't he have plans afterwards?'

He didn't say. He just asked me to go to his prom. We will talk about it when he picks me up from school. I will see you later Mom, I love you.

'I love you too, she said and hung up.

I dialed Pooch and got his voice mail. 'Hey Babe, I know that you're probably in the shower right now, but I need to tell you that there's a change in plans for tonight.

Brandon's girl is sick, and he asked me to go to the prom with him. He can't take anyone else because he doesn't want to hurt her feelings by showing up there with someone she knows. He's picking me up after school so call me at about 12:30PM. Talk to you later. I hung up and raced out of the door to catch my bus.

'Mikasa? Mikasa?'

The teacher was calling my name, but I was daydreaming about Pooch. It was my last class, and I couldn't get him off my mind. It didn't make sense that I liked him so much in such a short amount of time. I focused on Mr. Browns' face and answered the question without thinking about it as the bell rang. I gathered my things and headed for the door.

'Goodbye Mr. Brown.' He watched me leave with a puzzled look on his face. I must have answered right because he was one of the teachers that got a kick out of embarrassing students when they were wrong. I walked outside and saw the pretty A8 gleaming in the sun with Pooch and Brandon resting on it talking. They both smiled at me with dreamy eyes and said hello as I approached them.

Hi Pooch. I left you a message this morning. You didn't have to come for me today.

'Don't worry I got your message Mikasa. I figured that you would still need a ride. I'm accustomed to seeing you every day and after missing Wednesday I was determined to see you.'

You're something else Pooch. I just can't say it enough, and I apologize again for spoiling our plans. Don't even tell me what you had in store for me, or I will take it out on Brandon all night!

Brandon interjected. "Again, man I apologize too, I can't believe that my girl got so sick."

'Mikasa it is not a problem. I told Brandon that anything that I planned for us could be done another day. I'm flexible and I don't mind hanging out with you two until it is time for the prom. I didn't get to go to my prom so it will be nice to see you dressed up and I can get a few pictures of you to put in my house and my office.'

Man, I thought to myself. Is this man real? He is so fine, intelligent, thoughtful, and well mannered. And suddenly Brandon is being nice to him, finally.

Okay my nail salon is right up the block from here and Tammy will see me at 2PM for my hair. Do you have the dress, Brandon?

"It's in the trunk Mikasa along with your first pair of red bottoms."

What! Daddy is going to kill you! You know that I don't wear high heels like that, and you also know that he promised to get my first pair of Christian Louboutin's.' Tsk, let me see them.

"Let's go Mikasa, I will show them to you in the car. I called your mother before I picked them out. She gave me permission to buy them for you." Brandon reached into the trunk and took out the shoe box. He got in the back seat and got comfortable.

I got in and said, 'Well Daddy will still be pissed because you didn't ask him. He would've said no anyway. Pass me the box.

Brandon held the box and passed me one shoe. I gasped. The shoe in my hand was the one that I'd been gushing over for months in the Vogue magazine that was in my room. The shoe was completely encrusted with rhinestones with a 4-inch heel.

You're so nosy boy! You saw these in the book in my room, didn't you? I love them they're so hot, and they will look so nice on me but Daddy…

"Listen Mikasa, it is just for one night then you can tuck them away until you grow up."

Grow up? You're a funny boy! Do not forget who is older here. What color is the dress?

"The dress is white."

What color is your suit?

"Well, I have a white one and I have a grey one. I will see which one looks better with your dress."

You're so flashy boy, I swear. Why are we wearing white? It is a prom not a wedding.

And I love the shoes by the way; they're so flashy, but I love them.

"We have to be the baddest couple there. Everyone is talking about wearing this color or that and the guys are renting tuxedos and regular suits. You know that my suit is a custom fit, and you will see that no one else will be wearing your dress. It is bad. You will see it when you get home. And I will apologize to Uncle Darius, but I just had to get you the shoes to thank you for doing this for me. It means so much to me and thanks for leaving that book around. It made it quite easy to shop for you. Expensive but easy, and you're worth every dollar. Thanks so much Cuz."

I smiled still admiring the shoes. Once we parked Pooch took the shoe and looked at it. 'This is hot. How much were they?'

We got out of the car as Pooch handed him the shoe to put in the box. He popped the trunk so that Brandon could put it back in the trunk.

"They were about a grand." He said it like he was talking about a dollar. I glanced at Mikasa thinking that it was excessive for cousin-to-cousin gift, but the sheer joy on her face over them kept me quiet.

We walked into the salon and Candi greeted us and took me back to the pedicure station. I motioned to Pooch and they both came towards me, but Brandon sat in the chair beside me to get his feet done too. Pooch sat across from me as we talked about his day and what we would do over the weekend. He was always so secretive about where he was taking me, so he didn't give any specific details about where we would go. Once the French pedicure set, I moved up to the nail station. Brandon's nails were being buffed at this point. Pooch pulled out his wallet to pay for everything and Candi pointed to my cousin.

'He paid already.'

He tried to put a twenty on the table as a tip, but she said, 'He paid that too.'

I smiled at Brandon as Pooch nodded at him. After about an hour we left the nail salon and headed for Tammy's' shop. When we entered the shop Brandon said, 'Oh Cuz, could you please get loose curls pinned up because the dress is strapless. I mean if you don't mind. I bought you a necklace and I thought that you could show it off on that pretty neck of yours.'

Pooch looked at me as I looked at him and I said, 'Sure Brandon." Why don't you go to the Bodega and get me a sandwich and a bottle of lemonade? Give us just a few moments alone.

"Alright what about you Pooch, you want something?"

Just get a foot long and we will share it, I said.

Pooch nodded at Brandon and looked at me. While Tammy washed my hair Pooch said, 'Your cousin is going all out for this isn't he? A thousand-dollar pair of shoes for one night, man, I can't wait to see your dress. He is setting the bar high. Are you sure that he is just your cousin and I heard you say that you were older earlier. How old did you say he was again?'

Stop playing, you know that he is my cousin and I told you that he's only fourteen. I don't understand why he's spending all this money for one night and I have a feeling that Daddy isn't going to like it at all. My baby cousin can be so extravagant.

'And he is only fourteen? Doesn't high school begin at fourteen?'

Usually, but he's in the eleventh grade already. My aunt never had him tested but I suspect that he's a genius. And he is her only child, so she spoils him rotten. I still get allowance at sixteen, he has a debit card with God knows how much limit, so a thousand dollars means nothing to him. There is such a double standard in my family, and it's unfair to me. I imagine if I were a boy my father would give me much more space and privileges but since I'm a girl everything costly comes from my father or else, I don't get it. So, I already know that I'm going to get an earful about the shoes and even him paying for my hair and nails. You see how my father is with me and he already feels like Brandon takes advantage of our relationship.

Tammy pinned the last curl in place as Brandon returned. Pooch pulled out his wallet again and again his payment was refused.

"He paid this morning."

We both glanced at Brandon as Pooch complimented Tammy's' work.

'She looks awesome,' Pooch said as he gently kissed my lips. Tammy looked at Pooch and Brandon with a confused look on her face.

Tammy, he's my cousin.

She smiled and waved as we left the salon.

When we got in the car Brandon handed me the sandwich and drink.

"Pooch, please drop me off at my house so that I can prepare for tonight. I have an appointment with the massage therapist at 4pm. Mikasa, would you like a massage too?"

Boy you are bugging! No thank you. I laughed at him. You really think that you are royalty, don't you? You're so spoiled boy!

"Whatever Mikasa; like you aren't spoiled too! My uncle keeps you and Auntie laced and wanting for nothing. I'm just following his lead."

After Pooch put his address in the GPS Brandon continued.

"As soon as you get in the house please try on the dress. I need to know if you are pleased with my choice. I still have time to get you something else if you're not. I will pick you up at 7:30pm okay?"

That's fine Brandon. That will give Pooch and I some time to relax. What's the plan after prom?

"I have tickets for this mixed dance event at the W Hotel, but I know that I'm already imposing on you enough so just going to the prom will be fine."

Pooch glanced over at me expressing that he was okay with it.

We will see how I feel in those heels. We just might make it to the W tonight.

After dropping Brandon off Pooch and I headed straight to my house. We parked and I grabbed the shoebox and my bag as Pooch picked up the extra-long garment bag. We went into the house, and I called my mom. She picked up on the first ring.

'Hello?'

Hi Mom. Pooch and I are at the house. My hair, nails and toes are done, and I'm going to try the dress on now. If it fits, we will just chill here until it is time to go tonight if that is okay.

"That's fine baby, I trust you."

Thank you, Mom, and thanks for the shoes.

'Huh? Oh yes, I gave Brandon permission to purchase the shoes but of course he paid for them.'

He bought me red bottoms Mom. They were a thousand dollars.

There was silence on the line, and I knew that Mommy wasn't happy.

'Your Dad is going to lose it; you know that don't you? And I'm going to get Brandon. He didn't tell me that he was buying Louboutin's. Just wait until I see him.'

So, Mommy, when am I getting my debit card? You know that Brandon has one.

'That's a conversation for another time. I will see you in a while baby girl.'

Okay, bye Mom.

Make yourself comfortable while I try on this dress. Here is the remote for the television and sound system. I will be right back.

I went into my bedroom and laid the garment bag across the chaise. I placed the shoe box on the floor and stepped out of my sandals. After taking off my tee shirt and jeans I unzipped the bag. I was not prepared for the beauty of the strapless Ivory Dutch Satin sheath with the simple flounce at the hem. I lifted it out of the bag and found a replica of the same dress in another size, size eight. Size six was in my hand.

My goodness, this boy is thorough. I tried the size six first. I couldn't find my strapless bra, so I held it up around my breasts and looked in the mirror. Wow, this looks good. I stepped into my fancy shoes and walked carefully into the living room holding the dress up in two places. I turned with my exposed back to Pooch.

Zip me up please.

He paused and looked at me as if I was the most beautiful girl that he had ever seen. He took his time zipping me up and admiring me all at once.

'You look so good girl.'

I smiled. "Thank you, I feel awesome!"

I turned completely around before facing him.

'You look amazing, and your waist is so tiny!'

Thank you. I didn't even think that I could fit a size six, but this feels good, and it looks amazing, but it is a wedding dress. This is a little much for a prom don't you think? Not to mention that it was also tabbed in my book as my future wedding dress, and it cost $9,000.00. He needs to get something else. Let me get him on the phone.

I dialed and he picked up on the first ring. I put him on the speakerphone.

Hi B, the dress fits, but it's too expensive, and it's a wedding dress.

'Pooch, are you there man?'

"I'm here. What's up?"

'How does it look? Will we kill it tonight or what? Your call.'

"It's working man. She looks royal. She is gorgeous in this dress."

'Okay that's what I was going for. Mikasa, I know that you like the dress. I don't care how much it costs. I don't care if you never wear it again. My only concern is for you to be comfortable in it. That's why I bought two sizes to ensure your comfort. Tonight is my night and the least that I could do is make you feel like the princess that you are. We're family and there's not a thing in this world that's too good for you. If it's okay with you, I want you to keep it, wear it tonight and I will see you after seven, okay?'

"But B, you're spending too much on me for this. Daddy is going to flip."

'Mikasa it's one night, and it is my prom so he should understand and we only live once. I am cool with it, and you know that my mother doesn't care, and it's her money so just roll with me on this okay. You look good; I will look good; it's my night baby, thanks for making it special already by saying yes. See you later?'

All Right.

'Later Pooch."

"Later, Pooch responded."

As soon as he hung up my dad called.

'Mikasa?'

Hey Dad, how are you?

'Do you really want to know Mikasa? Not so good. Your cousin couldn't find anyone else to take to his prom? All these girls are chasing him down and he's monopolizing your time again? Why didn't you call me Mikasa?'

I looked over at Pooch and sighed.

"I'm sorry Daddy. Kim is sick and believe it or not they're dating exclusively so he didn't want to take another girl. You know that I've been teaching him to dance for months so he's comfortable with me."

'He's dating exclusively. Do you know how crazy that sounds! He is only fourteen years old, and you are his cousin Mikasa. You and I both know what happens on prom night and he can't keep his hands off you on a regular day. What makes you think that he will control himself tonight? What is he supposed to do with all that pent up energy that he has? Why didn't you call me?'

"Daddy please I don't need to hear all of that, and I told him that you would be mad. He can't help it if the girl is sick Daddy."

'You know what you're right he can't help it and you don't have to go. And what do you mean you told him that I would be mad? He doesn't answer to me Mikasa, you do. Instead of telling him that I would be mad you should have called me and told him that you couldn't go.'

"But Daddy!"

'Mikasa! Let me speak to Pooch.'

"What makes you think that he's here Dad?"

'Don't play with me girl, put him on the phone. Your mother already told me that he's there.

I handed Pooch the phone and motioned for him to unzip me. He did so, carefully, and quietly. I went to my room to change.

"Hello Mr. Jones."

'Hello Pooch. Do you remember what we discussed? Don't make any moves on my daughter. I'm giving you some space today considering the circumstances. Do you understand?'

"Yes, sir I do."

 I don't believe this boy; what is he up to? What time are they leaving for this prom?'

"Around 7:30PM."

'I will see you then. Can you pass the phone back to my daughter?'

Pooch handed me the phone at my bedroom door.

'Mikasa?'

Yes, Daddy.

'Do not leave tonight before I see you. Do you understand?'

Yes.

Goodbye Mikasa.

What did he say to you Pooch?

Pooch stared at me intently but didn't respond.

Pooch?

'Mikasa, I have to stay in your fathers' good graces to keep seeing you. There are certain things that he says to me that he doesn't expect to be repeated.'

"So, you won't tell me?"

'Do you want to continue seeing me Mikasa?'

What does that have to do with any......?

'Do you like me?'

Of course, I like you and I want to continue seeing you. You're here with me now.

'Do you want to continue seeing me?'

I sighed again. Yes, I said yes.

I stepped up to him and kissed him. He stopped me and kissed my shoulder and my neck. He returned to my lips; kissed me again and then he sat down. I stood there for a moment savoring the kiss and then I went to the kitchen to pour the drink and cut the sandwich in two. I brought them out to Pooch and set them on the tray. We watched television, ate, and drank lemonade. And then he spoke.

'I can tell you something though. You were right about one thing. Your Dad isn't happy.'

"I know and I feel bad about it. Brandon always brings the drama. He's the only person that my parents always argue about, and I hate to upset my dad. I thought that my mom would be able to smooth this out with him, but it seems as if I just got her in trouble with my dad over this too and where is she? I'm surprised that my mom isn't home now. I better start getting ready, it's 6pm.

I went to the bathroom, and I took a warm shower to prevent my curls from dropping. As I stepped out to air dry, I heard Mommy come in the house. I wrapped the towel around my body and entered my bedroom. After thoroughly applying the French shimmer lotion to my entire body I laid on the bed to air dry again. I put on my ivory lace panties; spritzed the air with Gucci parfum and stepped through the scent twice. I put on my ivory satin robe and sat at the vanity mirror to put on my diamond earrings from Daddy. I checked my face and Mom came into my room.

'You look pretty and smell so good.'

I thanked her as she kissed my cheek, and I kissed back then she spoke.

'Come in my room so that I can clean up your eyebrows.'

I followed and sat as my mother skillfully arched my eyebrows, applied mascara to my lashes, applied her favorite lipstick to my lips and lightly dusted my face. She told me to open my eyes and I was in shock.

Makeup Mom: wow, thank you. I love it!

We returned to my room, and she helped me into my dress. She glanced at the price tag as she snipped it off. 'This is nice Mikasa, and it looks amazing on you.' I could hear the concern in her voice as she zipped me up.

Can you believe that it's a six? All my clothes are size eight. I didn't realize that my waist was so small until I put this gown on.

'You really look beautiful she said as her eyes filled up. My baby has grown up.'

I stepped into my shoes, and she said, 'The shoes are pretty, but the heels are high, and your dad is going to be really pissed. I'm kind of mad too. I wanted to go with Darius to get your first pair. These are bad.' She wiped her eyes as we walked into the living room.

When Pooch saw me enter the room this time he was at a loss for words, he took a few pictures, then the doorbell rang, and it was Brandon. He entered the house wearing an Ivory Armani suit with an Ivory shirt, Peach and Ivory tie and kerchief, diamond cuff links and ivory snakeskin shoes. He was immaculate. He had three boxes in his hand.

"Hello Auntie, what do you think?" He said this and turned completely around very slowly so that Mom could admire him from every angle.

'Boy if Pooch weren't here, I would really air your tail out, but we will discuss exactly what I think later. You look handsome but I would have preferred it if you didn't purchase wedding attire for your prom.' Brandon's' eyes were glued on Mikasa, and he didn't respond to me.

"Man, Pooch was not lying when he said you looked royal girl you're wearing the heck out of that dress. That's the size six, right?"

'Boy I know that you hear me talking to you! Focus on me and answer me. You know that this is wedding attire. What will we do when Mikasa gets married, and those shoes! You want Darius to lose it, don't you?'

"Auntie no worries, we can wear this to Mikasa's' wedding." Instantly my mothers' jaw dropped, I was shocked, and Pooch was wearing an "I knew it" expression all over his face but Brandon smirked and said, just kidding just kidding!

But the look on Pooch's' face said that he knew better.

"You know my style by now Auntie, I have to be the baddest man in the room, and Mikasa has to look the part too, so here we are."

'But Brandon, is all this necessary for one night? Two nine-thousand-dollar dresses, a thousand-dollar pair of shoes?'

I know that it's just one night, but it's a special night for me. I only have one prom, so I had to do it up. I apologize for the high heels but I knew how much Mikasa wanted them so I took a chance and got them, and I will personally apologize to Uncle Darius. I really don't want to upset him; it's just that all my boys are wearing colors so I figured that we would really stand out in wedding white. Please forgive me Auntie!"

He looked at my mother with puppy dog eyes and a smile trying to win her over, but it was not working tonight. He stepped towards me with the boxes, opened the top one and slid the corsage on my wrist. There were two beautiful orchids and one remained in the box for him. He handed the box to my mom with a smile and opened the smaller jewelry box first. He removed an icy diamond tennis bracelet and put it on my other wrist. It was so clear that it was blinding to look at. He opened the other box removing a matching icy diamond necklace. Mom tried to hide her displeasure but said, "The jewelry is beautiful; it looks so real!"

Brandon smiled and said, 'It's real Auntie I would never buy Mikasa anything that isn't real, and doesn't it look pretty on her?'

Now Mom was so aggravated, and it showed. 'Turn towards me and let me put this flower on you boy. Just how much did you spend on your cousin today?

"I'm not sure Auntie. I probably spent a little over thirty-five including the jewelry. I could have …

'Brandon really? Did you have to spend so much money for one night? Does your mother know you spent all this money on Mikasa alone?'

"It was for Kim, but you know that my mother could care less about how much I spent, and if I tell her, it's for Mikasa now she will be fine with that. She is her favorite and only niece."

'You are really trying my patience Brandon and Darius is on his way here now. I have defended you for years, but you are on your own tonight.

Just when I think that you are maturing and trying to find your own way you're still clinging to Mikasa.' Mommy paused, closed her eyes and apologized to Pooch for the outburst.

"Can we wait outside for Uncle D if you do not mind Auntie? I also would like to get a picture of Mikasa outside before we leave."

For the first time ever, I heard my mother suck her teeth as she looked at her phone. 'Go ahead Brandon just don't try to escape before her father gets here do you understand?'

"I do Auntie."

Brandon displayed confidence in himself that I hadn't seen before, and I was shocked and regretted my decision to accompany Brandon to his prom.

We all left the house and Mom locked the door. When I got outside, I couldn't believe that a white-on-white Maybach was sitting outside with the driver. It was the most beautiful car that I had ever seen but it all felt very awkward since Mommy was upset.

Brandon caught my reaction and smiled but my mother and Pooch were visibly disturbed by the extravagance but said nothing. The driver stepped out of the car and held the door ajar, but Brandon signaled to him, and he closed the door and stood beside it. We posed for a few pictures then Daddy drove up. He got out of the car and walked over to me to hug me, touched Pooch's' shoulder to acknowledge him and put his hands around Brandon's' throat so quickly that it took us all a moment to react. Brandon was in shock as my mother tried to pry my fathers' hands from around his throat.

'We can't do this out here Darius, please! They're going to the prom, and they will be back at midnight. We can deal with him in the house then. He is our nephew. Please Darius, calm down. They will be in a room full of people Mikasa will be fine, please Darius, please baby don't do this here.'

The three of us pulled at my father as my mother spoke softly to him in his ear. I could feel the heat of my fathers' rage and slowly he began to respond and loosen his grip. Pooch had a good hold of my dad and as soon as he released his hands from Brandon's' throat Mom pushed Brandon towards the car and motioned for me to follow.

Daddy was still in a rage mumbling something that I couldn't understand, as Pooch continued to hold him on one side and my mother held the other side. I was embarrassed and mad at myself for putting Daddy through this and mad at Brandon for causing this confusion. Brandon pulled me gently towards the car and we got in and drove off as Pooch helped my mother get my dad into the house.

## POOCH

As I helped Mikasa's mother get her husband in the house I was feeling what he felt. Of course, something was very wrong with Brandon's' relationship with Mikasa and I guess that it hadn't been addressed until this moment. Darius just assaulted Brandon: Mikasa's' mother was crying, and Darius was yelling something like he can't have my daughter, he can't have my daughter.

Once we were all in the house and Mr. Jones had calmed down a bit, Mikasa's mother thanked me for helping her and apologized profusely for what had just happened. She wished that I hadn't seen all of that and told me that I could come back at midnight to see Mikasa when she returned. I wanted to stay to try to get an understanding of what just happened, but I sensed that they needed to be alone right now.

'It's quite all right Mrs. Jones; I pray that everything will be all right. I will see you later.'

I left their house with a million thoughts running through my mind and none of them made me feel comfortable. I thought back to when I met up with Mikasa and Brandon at school earlier today and I was surprised that Brandon was so polite to me. He was nothing like he had been the other day at brunch. He didn't seem to be a bad guy but when Mikasa walked up his energy instantly changed. I could feel the attraction that he felt toward her, and it really made me uncomfortable and angry. At the salon, in the car, at the house; I sensed his possessiveness over Mikasa in the tone and content of his conversation. He was gushing over her, so infatuated with his own cousin and not hiding it from anyone anymore.

I struggled to maintain my composure because I never wanted my temper to come between Mikasa and I, but seeing the shoes and dress that he bought for her was just too sexy a purchase for a first, second or third cousin. Who shops for their female cousin alone and what fourteen-year-old boy knows anything about Vera Wang or any other type of girls' fashion?

It was apparent to me at that moment that he studied Mikasa and knew everything that she liked. He also was playing her mother against her father and didn't care if he pissed either of them off anymore. If it was pleasing to Mikasa he would give anything to her regardless of the consequences. All of it was mind boggling. Hard to fathom.

And if seeing them in wedding attire wasn't enough to push Mikasa's father over the edge, the Maybach waiting for them was the icing on the cake that threw him into instant rage towards Brandon.

 I wouldn't want to be in Mikasa's' father shoes right now as I'm unsteady in my own as the new boyfriend.  Brandon was a problem and if he would go this far to please Mikasa what else was he capable of?

I'm very uneasy about her being alone with him tonight.  Even though they will be in a place with a room full of people when he sees Mikasa he blocks everyone and everything else out.  To me, this puts Mikasa in a very precarious position because she knows and loves the little cousin that she helped to raise but she doesn't seem to know how to react to the person he has become.

 So, what do I do now? If I follow them, I become the possessive man that she may begin to resent and if I don't, I will worry and stress over the next four hours. Man, I wish my parents were here now. My Dad would have the answer to all of this. I wish that I could talk with him right now.

## DARIUS

Patti, how the hell could you let this happen? Did you see that boy with my daughter dressed like he was getting married? How could you Patti?!

I have loved and trusted you all these years and you let this boy buy my daughter jewels, a gown, shoes and that car! This is your watch, Patti! Why would you give that boy permission to shop for and wife my daughter? That is my daughter Patti. Do you understand her worth and your own? How could you call me and tell me this after you okayed it! This is your fault, Patti. You're always babying that boy and now at fourteen he's trying to move like a grown ass man with my daughter! I have been telling you this for years!!!!!!!!!!!!!!

Your nephew is sick, and you signed off on this and your degenerate sister cosigned it. Get her on the phone. I want to speak to her right now. Get her ass on the phone!

'Listen, just stop yelling! You don't think that I feel terrible about this Darius? Do you really think that I would sell *our daughter* out like that? She is his cousin, and he is OUR nephew I…

He is your nephew, Patti. I don't want ANY credit for that. He has always had an unnatural attraction to my daughter that you and your sister thought was so cute. And today with your own eyes and mine I see my daughter and **YOUR** nephew dressed in wedding whites, she has jewelry on that I didn't buy, that I know you didn' buy either and you let him pay for her hair and nails and the shoes! How does that sound or feel right to you Patti? I mean, just call your sister. I hate what this boy does to us! Damn it. We are always arguing about this boy and my daughter Patti. Aren't you tired of this? Call your sister!

Patti dialed her sister twice and she didn't answer her cell but when she dialed the office, she answered on the first ring.

"Angle Advertising, Sara speaking."

Sara, this is Darius, what the hell is wrong with you?

"Darius, why are you calling here? This is a business; my business and you made your choice."

'What in the world are you talking about woman? We are your family, and I am calling to see why your son has my daughter at the prom with him. Why did you allow him to buy her shoes, a dress and diamonds for a prom that last four hours and why does a fourteen-year-old need a Maybach for his prom Sara?'

"What are you talking about? I didn't even know that Mikasa went with him tonight but so what we are family, what's the problem?"

'What's the problem?! The problem is that proms are for people that are not related. People have sex on prom night, and you know as well as I do that your son is infatuated with my daughter. If he does anything to my daughter I….

"You're so old-fashioned Darius! Brandon has a crush on Mikasa and if he wants to spend money on her I don't have a problem with that. It's just money! I buy Mikasa stuff, he buys Mikasa stuff. No biggie. And the Maybach is something he asked me about months ago, so I leased it for him. He bought her some expensive things and you're really bent out of shape about it aren't you? Are you the only one who can buy my niece and sister expensive things? Well, just act like it is all from me. It is my money, remember?

He loves his cousin. There isn't anything wrong with that. You're just mad that someone besides you is spoiling your daughter, but we are family remember? You said that at the beginning of the conversation, and you know that as family my son will not do anything to your precious Mikasa so lighten up."

I sighed and gritted my teeth. Now I see where the madness stems from. I hung up the phone. How could Patti be so intelligent and normal, and her sister be so sick in the head! I paced the floor and Patti continued to try to soothe me, but I put my hand up.

'Please Patti I can't be touched right now. Your sister… if I never ever see your sister again it would be too soon.

'Darius please just listen to me for a minute. I apologize I'm pissed, shocked, embarrassed and I'm no longer in denial about my nephews' feelings for OUR daughter. He loves her, I know it. I can see now that the talk that we had last weekend and the time that we spent together didn't impact him at all and I accept all the blame for this. I didn't want to lose it in front of Mikasa's company, but I obviously should have. I can't even imagine how he is feeling right now. I hate to admit it, but I was just too embarrassed to react. I really hate myself right now for what I just put you through and I'm sure that Mikasa is blaming herself right now for putting you through it too. She looked sick when you grabbed him.'

Where are they Patti?

'Please Darius there are too many people down there, you cannot just barge in there!

Patti please, I just want to know.'

'Marina Del Ray.'

Okay, call her in a few minutes and check on her, I have to use the bathroom.

# BRANDON

We arrived at the pier where most of my classmates were gathered and Mikasa was still shaken up. I touched her hand.

'Are you okay?'

She shook her head, and I stepped out and escorted her from the car. Of course, all eyes were on us. She looked so beautiful that it was difficult for me to keep my eyes off her, but I looked around and spoke to everyone as they congratulated me on my last game and general all-around performance. The compliments were raining down non-stop around us confirming that I had made all the right choices. We moved toward the dining area and our table and the faces of some of my boys came into view. When we got close one of them said, 'Damn baby boy you two are really doing it! But where's Kim?'

She is sick and you know that I couldn't come alone. This is Mikasa. Isn't she fine? Don't look too long though because I will cut you!

I smirked at him, but I was dead serious. We kept it moving and found our seats. I looked around, and yes, Mikasa outshined all the chicks in the room. Her skin was beautiful, her makeup was flawless, and the diamonds refracted light all around the ballroom. We got up to dance to slow music. There was only one couple on the floor, and they were teachers. Mikasa was distracted so I held her close and said, "Please forgive me Mikasa for upsetting your father. I guess I should have spoken to him instead of Aunt Patti before I asked you to come to the prom. I know he doesn't really like me so I was afraid that he would say no. I hate to see you like this.

'Don't worry about it Brandon. I will have to make it up to my dad somehow. Tonight is your night so let's try to enjoy it." I smiled on the outside trying to hold the turmoil that I felt within.

I didn't like to see Mikasa upset but I worked so hard to make everything perfect tonight and I really wanted to enjoy it. I tried to ease her mind with small talk.

Cuz, you know that every eye is on you in here, right? She smiled.

'It is your night baby boy. You know that they're clocking the all-star. They don't even know me.'

But they want to Cuz. You look gorgeous. Thanks again for coming tonight.

'We're family, cousins; we always have each other's back. But seriously, you know that you really didn't have to spend all this money on me. You're only fourteen years old and $35,000 is a lot to spend on someone for one night. Does Aunt Sara know how much you spent? I still don't understand how you got a debit card before me. I'm the older one here.'

Are you jealous of that Mikasa? You know that my mother doesn't care how much I spend, especially on you. And you don't need a debit card. Anything you want I got you. Just tell me and I will pick it up and bring it to you or we can go get it together. I nuzzled her ear with my nose and squeezed her tighter. She stiffened so I loosened my grip.

'I'm sorry Mikasa."

She relaxed and we continued to dance to several slow songs. We talked about basketball and fashion which were our two favorite topics and then I felt her bag vibrate against my back in her hand. When the song ended, she excused herself and went to the restroom. I did the same. I went in the stall to adjust my cup and when I came out Antoine pushed a flask in my face. I took it to the head, and it was sweet and fruity. I suddenly felt relaxed, and he grabbed his flask back and laughed.

'Dag, you drank it all! There was gin in there man.'

## MIKASA

I looked at my phone and there were two missed calls: Mom and Pooch. I pressed redial and heard his voice.

'Hey babe, I'm so sorry that you had to see that. Brandon is always upsetting my father. I'm afraid of what comes next. How's my dad?'

"Your mom is taking care of him so try not to worry about it right now. I'm sure that everything will work out. How are you? Is Brandon behaving himself?"

I heard the concern in his voice and the stress. I refused to let Brandon's actions anger another man in my life.

'Everything is fine Pooch. He's having the time of his life.  Everyone is showering us with so much attention like we are superstars. I thought that I saw one of Kim's friends, but she didn't come over to us. You know that I can't wait to see you later. My Mom called too so I'm going to call her now. Bye babe.

'Wait a minute, are you sure that you're, okay?'

Yes, I'm fine, just make sure that I see you tonight, okay? Goodbye.

'Bye.'

I dialed my house. Hi Mom, is Daddy, okay?

"Daddy is fine, how are you? Is Brandon behaving himself?"

'Yes Mom. He's enjoying himself. He apologized for upsetting Dad, but he didn't say a word about Dad almost choking him to death. I feel bad about what happened. I should have called Daddy first. I know that he feels like we are in cahoots when it comes to Brandon.  I really feel awful.'

'Mikasa you aren't to blame for any of this. I have allowed things to slide, and I even encouraged the closeness between you and Brandon for years. Your father and I will take care of Brandon together this time.  Things must change for your benefit as well as Brandon's. I want you to enjoy yourself tonight. You know that I love you baby girl, don't you?'

'Of course, Mommy, I love you too.'

"Daddy loves you too, see you later."

I ended the call and exited the bathroom. Brandon was standing right by the door. The DJ threw on a JayZ jam, and we were back on the dance floor. We danced for another hour then Brandon got restless.

## BRANDON

It was almost 10 o'clock and I noticed that Kim's bestie was grilling me, so I said, 'Mikasa let me take you to the W now. I know that you want to be home by midnight and it's nice over there. I'm over this crowd. We can dance with grown folks there and fit right in. You really helped me with the dance lessons. They cannot keep up with us in here.'

I smiled at Brandon. He was so smug at times.

"If you're ready to leave it is cool. I haven't been to the W so I'm sure it will be nice. Just let me go to the bathroom and then we can head out." I spotted the dude from earlier headed the same way. We entered the bathroom, and he pulled out the flask again. But he held it back this time. I handed him a twenty spot and he passed me the flask. I took it to the head and felt nice. I slipped a piece of gum in my mouth then I stepped out of the bathroom and of course this kid was all up in Mikasa's face. I grabbed her hand and he swiftly stepped back. We exited the Marina and the driver stepped out of the car to open the door for us. Once inside we sat back, and I pressed a button for the massage feature. The driver pulled off as I closed my eyes and moaned at the relaxing pulsating feeling across my back.

'How do you like the car Mikasa? I wanted the best one I could find for tonight.'

"It is nice B. The leather is so soft, and the music seems like we're at a live concert. You really went all out for tonight. You had all the tongues wagging in that place."

'Mikasa, you know that I love you right? I leaned in and rested my head on her shoulder breathing in her face.'

"Brandon what's that smell? What where you drinking?"

Huh? I had some fruit punch.

"Fruit punch? Your breath smells like something harder than fruit punch. You're only fourteen remember?"

'And you're sixteen, so what I'm a man now.'

Really, wait until I tell Mama.

Ssh.

He was slurring a bit now as he placed his finger to my lip.

You don't have to tell anyone. It is just fruit punch.

'You know that you don't have to drink to have fun Brandon.'

I know Mikasa. I just wanted to try something new tonight. Please don't tell your mama. I won't do it again, don't be upset.

His head remained on my shoulder, and he held my hand like he used to do when we were young.

'Did you enjoy your prom? Your suit looks nice on you, and we spent all of two hours showing it off in there. Did you have fun?'

"Thanks, Mikasa, and yes, I had a wonderful time there with you. Did you have a little fun? You know that we dance so well together, and we looked good girl. I had fun dancing with you."

'It was fun and nice to see you enjoying yourself and comfortable dancing. You never really needed the help anyway. You dance very well just like my Daddy.'

Oh, thanks Cuz. You smell so good. What are you wearing?

'The French perfume from Daddy.'

'That stuff is dangerous. I was trying to find something like it this morning, but I couldn't. I must have tested one hundred bottles of perfume, but nothing smelled quite like it. Umm.'

We rode in silence for another twenty minutes before reaching our destination.

The door opened and I stepped out to escort Mikasa from the car. Once again, all eyes were on us, and I felt so suave with her by my side looking so good. We entered the ballroom and people congratulated us thinking that we just got married.

They were stepping so I gently moved Mikasa onto the dance floor. We watched for a moment then began to mimic each move as Mikasa held the hem of her dress up a little.

I lead and Mikasa caught on so quickly that it felt magical.

'Wow, you're good at this. We never practiced and you're working it girl, look around.'

The couples formed a circle and danced around us admiring our moves. When the music stopped a couple approached us.

"Congratulations newlyweds you two look beautiful together, so sophisticated. If you don't mind us asking how old are you two?"

Mikasa laughed but I was grinning from ear to ear. 'We just came from my prom, we're not married. I am fourteen and she is sixteen.'

The couple looked us over in surprise.

"Your prom? That is some fancy attire for a prom. You two have excellent taste, very nice."

We thanked them for the compliment and continued to dance. We did a little tango; we waltzed, did some salsa moves and capped it off with a slow dance to the classic "Always and Forever". For a moment I lost myself as we danced, and I pulled Mikasa closer. She closed her eyes and rested her head on my shoulder with her face close to mine. My hand swiftly slipped over her butt as I kissed her lips. And then I felt her push me away.

'Brandon, what are you doing!' She quickly exited the ballroom.
I ran up behind her apologizing and reaching for her and she said, 'Let's go now Brandon before I make a scene up in here and don't touch me again!'

'Mikasa, come on now it's me, B.'

'Yes B, I know that it is you! I am your cousin; you aren't supposed to kiss me, and you definitely aren't supposed to feel my butt! What the hell is wrong with you?'

That was an accident. I just thought you were Kim for a minute. And we used to kiss all the time when were little, remember? Why are you tripping now?

'Why am I tripping? Just get in the car and take me home now. You just don't know when to quit. I want to see my man now so take me home. You're so out of control!

"Your man? You're with your man. That dude Pooch, he can't have you Mikasa. You belong with me and to me."

'What did you just say Brandon?'

I said that he can't have you!

'And what did you say before that?'

"I said that I'm your man. Yes, I said it. Do you think that I've loved and protected you all these years just so that another man could take you away from me?"

'Brandon, what the heck are you talking about? Did you bump your head, or did you have some X in that fruit punch? You're really tripping! Do you realize who I am? Is this the twilight zone? I'm Mikasa Jones, your first cousin, daughter of Patti and Darius Jones, niece of Sara who is your mother. Do you know who you are? I think we better go to the hospital because you have obviously lost your mind.'

"I know who you are, and I know exactly who I am, and I'm tired of hiding my feelings for you. I'm Brandon, your first cousin. I love you and you love me and a title; us being cousins shouldn't keep us from being together. I understand you; we are good together and I have the potential to provide for you better than any other man can, even your Daddy. Everything that you see here tonight is just a taste of what you can have with me. I can take care of you in every way Mikasa. If I can do all of this at fourteen just imagine when we, I mean I get that first eight figure contract!"

'Do me a favor please? Don't say another word.' I began to speak, and she reiterated, 'Do not say another word.'

I watched her in silence as she took off her corsage, the necklace and the bracelet.

'You're so lucky that I barely have anything on under this dress or else I would take it off too. How dare you do this to me? How could you? I've done nothing but love you like a little brother, and this is how you treat me?'

She tried to put the jewelry in my hand, but I wouldn't take it. I was smiling at the thought of her taking off the dress but then I spoke. Come on Mi…

'Shut up I told you that I don't want to hear another word from you, and I don't want to see you after tonight until you are normal again.'

I tried to speak but she looked at me as if she wanted to kill me.

'Don't do it!'

We pulled up in front of her house and she opened the door before the driver came to a complete stop. I moved to get out of the car and return the jewelry and corsage to her and she said, 'Don't get out, go home now Brandon!'

She threw the shoes on the seat, slammed the door and my heart sank.

## POOCH

I was sitting on Mikasa's porch when the car pulled up. So, I could see that she wasn't happy, and was arguing with him when she got out of the car. Her corsage and jewelry were curiously absent. I saw her toss the shoes in the car before slamming the door, so they were gone too, and she walked carefully looking as if she wanted to cry before she saw me. I stood up to walk towards her and her expression changed completely, and she smiled. She switched her mood up, turning on the sunshine.

'Hi Pooch.'

Hi babe, are you all right? What did he do?

'Nothing, I'm fine. He just got drunk and was talking crazy.'

Where is your corsage and the jewelry and why did you take off your shoes?

'My feet hurt, and I figured that my dad would be here. I didn't want that to get him going again. Let's just go inside so that I can change my clothes.

I held her for a moment and asked again.

Mikasa, you know that you can tell me anything don't you?

'Yes, I do Pooch. Just let me change. We can go somewhere and talk but I'm fine.'

As I held her, I knew that she was anything but fine. Her body was so tense, and her pulse was very quick. She opened the door, and her parents were on the couch. They both said hello and Mikasa went to her father and held him for a while sitting beside him. She whispered gently in his ear. Tears fell down her cheeks and his body began to relax. He held her head as she spoke to him. She said, 'I'm so sorry Daddy; please don't take this out on Mommy. She apologized again and tears continued to flow down her cheeks. She spoke softly to her dad, and I sat down across from her mom. Her mother mouthed to me, 'Is she alright?'

I nodded and we sat quietly as they had their moment. After a few more soft words were spoken, Mikasa sat back as her father wiped the tears from her face.

'Mommy I'm fine everything is okay. I just had to clear the air with Daddy before I did anything else tonight. I thought about him the whole time I was there, and I really felt bad about everything.'

"So where are your shoes and the jewelry?"

'I left all of it in the car. I didn't want to upset Daddy again over it. None of it is worth him being angry or getting arrested for killing Brandon. None of this is worth it. It was getting late, so we left the W to get back here on time. I will send the other dress back to him and take this one to goodwill after I have it drycleaned.

"The W, I thought that you went to the Marina?"

'He got bored with his prom and he had the tickets already for the W but don't get upset Daddy I knew about it in advance, and he asked me first.'

Darius wasn't happy about these added details, but he didn't press Mikasa. Her mother was relieved, but I was puzzled. Mikasa looked at her parents and said, "I just want to spend a little time with Pooch if it's okay and I will be back in two hours.'

Her parents responded at the same time, "Well as long as you're alright Mikasa you go ahead, and we will deal with the rest later."

She went to the room to change, and I sat on the couch.

## MIKASA

I stripped out of the dress and panties and showered for what seemed like forever trying to wash away the memory of my cousin kissing and touching me. I patted myself dry, moisturized my body and got dressed. I returned to the living room and grabbed Pooch's' hand.

My father glanced at Pooch as we left. We drove in silence, and I was deep in thought when Pooch said, "Do you want to go somewhere or just sit and talk? I can drive up to City Island by the beach and we can just park and talk."

Let's head to the beach to talk but I want you to remain calm regardless of what I tell you. You can't react the way my father did earlier. I can't handle that right now.

'Okay Mikasa.'

We continued in silence. When we got to the beach, we got out of the car, walked over to the bench and sat down. Pooch held my hands and looked into my eyes.

First let me apologize again for what happened earlier. I never should've agreed to go to the prom with Brandon without telling my dad about it first. He is always right about things, and I know that he has had reservations about Brandon spending time alone with me for years now. Despite that, I have always trusted Brandon but of course tonight he betrayed that trust.

I really can't understand what went wrong tonight. I guess the entire day started off wrong. At first Brandon shocked me when I came out of school today and he was so nice to you. You both were talking and laughing like friends do. He was so comfortable and polite to you that it put me at ease. Then at the nail salon and the hair salon I felt a little strange because I was prepared to pay for both services as I always do but it was for his prom, so when he paid, I thought that it was okay. Then I saw the dress that I imagined that I would wear at my wedding right in front of me purchased by Brandon and it felt weird. A nine-thousand-dollar dress for a prom is extravagant even for me and the fact that he saw it in the book in my room threw me for a loop.

Now add the shoes, the jewelry, the car; it was all too much for two cousins going to the prom. We danced, he drank something, we went to the W and then ....

Tears began to slide down my cheek as I closed my eyes. Pooch held me in his arms now and began to tense up.

We entered the ballroom, we danced, and people started to surround us. They thought we were newlyweds. I laughed, but he smiled proudly like he was really enjoying the moment and I said no, we went to prom. He is fourteen years old, and I am sixteen. Always and forever came on and we started dancing, I closed my eyes wishing that he was you and then...

And then he felt my butt and kissed me on the lips simultaneously. I closed my eyes for just a minute like I'm doing now, and he took advantage of me. I still can't believe that he did that.'

Pooch was quiet but I could feel the anger rise in his body.

'I pushed him off me and walked away from him and out of the ballroom. I was done and ready to go home and his response to my reaction was that he thought that I was Kim, that it was just an accident. I was so pissed and then he had the nerve to say that I really shouldn't make a big deal of it because we used to kiss all the time when we were kids.

At that point I should have called you and just let him leave by himself, but I figured that he wouldn't continue to be so irrational, and I really didn't want to get you riled up too, so we got in the car, and he continued to talk crazy. He said that he loved me and that I loved him, and cousin is just a title that shouldn't stop us from being together. When I told him that I wanted to see my man just take me home he had the audacity to say that he was my man and that you couldn't have me. He bragged that tonight was just a preview of how well he could provide for me.

At that point I just lost it and told him not to say another word. I took off the jewelry and the corsage and told him that I didn't want to see him until my normal cousin returned.'

At that point Pooch was hot. He wiped the tears from my eyes and said, 'You know that this isn't the end? Pooch paused for a long time; it seemed like an eternity and then he continued.

If he went this far it's not going to end well for him because he doesn't know how to control himself or respect the fact that you are cousins. How am I supposed to react to this Mikasa?'

I fought to stay calm because she was already upset.

Well, he still is my cousin, my mothers' only nephew so I don't know Pooch. Do you think that giving him an a** whupping will change his state of mind? A part of me would like you to but I know that it won't have any effect on him because he seems so determined. I felt like I was in the twilight zone when he was saying all that crap to me with a serious expression on his face.

You saw my father almost strangle him to death and do you think that he mentioned any of that in the car on the way to the prom? Not at all, it was like it never even happened.

'I wish that I could act surprised, but I knew the first time that I saw you that your cousin had a thing for you. I was so surprised to discover that he was your cousin. The way that he looks at you tells it all. If I could just put my hands on him for about five minutes I....'

Okay so what if you beat him and he doesn't change then what? You go to jail for assault, Daddy goes to jail for assault and Mommy, and I are left alone to deal with him. He is highly intelligent and crafty. I mean, it's frightening to think about how cunning he is. I understand your anger, I'm very angry too, but I also know my cousin. He is perched somewhere between insanity and reality, and I will not allow him to separate me from my father or you. I'm convinced now that he is trying to separate us from the both of you so that he can just be with us again.

'So, what do we do now?'

I know that it will be hard for you, but I want you to continue to focus on me and do your best not to react to Brandon. Everything with us is so new and despite how I feel about you we're still getting to know each other. Let's focus on us and let my father take care of the rest of it.

'Mikasa, you know that I like you girl, I am beyond that and want to think and respond rationally but he touched you Mikasa, why can't I touch him?'

Listen; is it safe to say that we are in a relationship now?

'Yes, we are.'

Well, I want to be able to see you, and touch you and kiss you. I don't want anything or anyone to come between us. I made a bad decision today. I agreed to something that almost cost my father his freedom and my mother a load of pain. For a moment, I fell for a pair of shoes and my cousins' smile and after today my family will never be the same again. I lost what I thought was my best friend and brother today. So many things are running through my mind and all of it is killing me, but my goal was to get back to you tonight and here we are. You're my safe place. Please promise me that you will always be that safe place for me and don't tell my father what happened tonight please?

'Mikasa, what are you trying to do to me girl! How could I not agree to that? Of course, I will always be your safe place but what am I supposed to do when someone hurts you? How do I protect you? And not tell your father?'

Just love me and let it go.

'That's easy to say but are you going to let it go? You can't blame yourself for what happened today. You loved and trusted your cousin and he betrayed you. That's his cross to bear not yours. If you agree to love me and let it go, I will do the best that I can to move on from here, but I know that it will not be easy to see him and not do anything. I will try it your way though.'

I thought to myself, 'My woman and her cousin, man!'

## BRANDON

I'm in my bed right now and I don't even know how I got here. I'm fully clothed, and my head is pounding. Damn. I can see my phone vibrating on the desk, but I don't feel like answering it.

But what if it is Mikasa, I ask myself. I try to get up, but my head won't let me. I will call her later when I get up. I drifted back to sleep with my clothes on. A vision of Mikasa in white floated by in my dreams.

## Chapter 8 - PATTI

'Thank God our daughter is all right. I was praying that she would come home without incident so that we could move on from here. Like I said before I completely understand your anger and accept the blame for all of this, it's just that I tried to make up for what Sara didn't give that boy. He came into this world innocent and blameless and now we are all that he really has in this world. He's fourteen and Sara could really care less about the boy so you might as well say that I'm the boys' mother and I know that you resent that but what do we do now?'

I looked at my husband trying to reason with him. His head was in his hands, and he looked as if he was returning to the dark place that he was in earlier on in the evening.

"I have to be honest with you Patti I still want to harm him, and I'm so angry at you right now that I, I want to squeeze and shake you. Damn.

You hurt me so bad, the first time, so many years ago when you left me and took my daughter with you. And then you replaced me with your nephew and acted like I never even mattered in your life. You tried to get me to father the boy along with Mikasa and I still couldn't stop loving you even though I resented you for it. You fought me tooth and nail for the sake of that boy, but you never tried to understand why I made the mistake that I did. It feels as if our entire life consists of Brandon and his issues and now you are asking me what next?

If I could find a way not to love you Patti, I swear that I would right now, this minute. What do we do now? Well, let's see. If I remove him from the planet, you won't love me anymore but if I don't how do I look myself and Mikasa in the eye? She's my daughter, and it is my job to keep her from stuff like this."

'I know that it is your job to protect our daughter and an apology won't cover what I did to you so many years ago, but I do apologize for everything. For breaking up with you, for leaving, for not trusting you sooner, for forcing Brandon on you when I knew that you wanted your own son.

I was scared and selfish and I apologize Darius but how could you ever think that I replaced you with Brandon? I could never replace you with a little boy! I just tried to forget what we had by focusing on raising Mikasa and him and it has never been enough. I never stopped loving you even when I tried to date to forget you. I know that we argue all the time about him, but you have to understand that getting rid of Brandon will not solve this problem. Mikasa will have to carry that around for the rest of her life because no matter what she will think that you did it and she will wear that guilt like a chain around her neck for the rest of her life. So, why don't we do this? Let's have a talk with Brandon tomorrow with a therapist to see if we can work something out. I know a doctor who will see us on short notice. I called her earlier when I found out that Brandon asked Mikasa to go to the prom with him.'

"A therapist; really? So, you do understand how serious it is."

'Oh yes, I see it clearly now. I also think that Mikasa should move in with you until she goes to college so that she doesn't feel like she has to see Brandon anytime soon. I'm afraid that he's mentally unstable now and I really don't want him to go over the edge and try to harm or take her. I know that I'm asking for a lot, but can we agree that we have to help him? Can we do this together now?'

Darius sighed and paced the floor.

'He is a good kid Darius. He has so much promise aside from this. Mikasa will be in college in two months. Please help me with this. I can't do this by myself. I don't want to do this by myself.

"He's a good kid Patti! Really! Why, because he's your blood, he's smart and can play ball?" He sighed in frustration.

Now you are saying you want help. Does that mean that you want me back in your life for good or that you just want to work through this crisis together? What are you saying to me Patti?

## BRANDON

Mikasa is in my arms. We are dancing, smiling, and having a good time. She looks good; she smells good, just tell me that I'm not dreaming. I finally have her to myself I kiss her and now I hear banging, banging, banging in my dream. Who and what is banging in my dream? I turn over and lay on my back willing myself back into the dream, but the banging continues.

It's the door. I fumble around in the dark and look at the clock. It's four in the morning who is banging at my door!

I fling off my suit jacket and tie and walk to the door. I yank the door open, and it's Kim at my door waving her phone in my face. I pulled her through the door so fast that her heads spins and she loses her footing a bit.

'What the hell are you doing here Kim?'

She shoves her phone in my face displaying a picture. "Who is this?"

'It's me and Mikasa dancing at the prom.'

"Mikasa, who the hell is Mikasa?"

I'm pissed now. My head is pounding, she is questioning me, and I don't answer to anyone, especially not her.

'WHO DO YOU THINK YOU'RE TALKING TO!' I yell.

'Mikasa is my cousin.' I stared back at her defiantly daring her to continue.

Her tone softened, and she said "Your cousin? Didn't you call me and break our prom date together because you were sick? You sure don't look sick in this picture and that damn sure don't look like your cousin. Why would you play me like that Brandon? You know how I feel about you! Why would you do this to me?"

'I am going to ask you again why are you here? I was nice enough to call you and break our date, I should have just stood you up.'

"Stood me up I thought that you loved me Brandon we have been dating for 4 months!"

'Love you? I never said that I loved you. You jumped on my lap on our first date and gave it up like you were dating me for years. You're a freak Kim, and I don't want to see you anymore. How much was your dress?'

She was crying now and trying to hug me, but I wouldn't let her. I asked her again.

'How much was your dress, your hair and nails? Give me the total of everything?'

I had my wallet now and I took out five hundred.

"What are you talking about Brandon? What about our relationship? I don't understand what's happening. We didn't have any problems before the prom now you're flipping on me?"

'I'm not interested in you Kim I never was. You're a pretty girl; you can find yourself another baller and I'm sure that someone else on the team would like to have you then you can have a baller again. I won't ask again. How much did you spend?'

"Nine hundred dollars, she said."

'I laughed and pulled out another five hundred and put it all in her hand. Take it all and lose this address and my phone number. And when you see me, please don't speak. I'm over you so get over me, please.'

I showed her to the door, she walked out, and I slammed it. I went to my room and took off my pants. My head was still pounding as I looked at my phone. I noticed that I had twenty missed calls from Kim, so I deleted them all without listening to any of them. I took off my shirt and noticed the jewelry and corsage on my dresser. I thought to myself for a minute. What happened last night? I remembered the prom and all the attention on me and Mikasa. I also remember the W Hotel and the couple who thought Mikasa, and I were newlyweds. I couldn't help but smile at that memory. I can remember dancing to "Always and Forever" holding Mikasa in my arms. And now I'm here. My head is pounding, my throat is dry, and I wish that she was here with me.

## MIKASA

I got in the house at 2AM on the dot. My mom and dad were still sitting on the couch where I left them. They both spoke to me, and Dad got up. 'Goodnight Mikasa, I will see you tomorrow. 'Patti, I'm heading home. Call me tomorrow and I will come and pick you up. Pooch let me speak to you for a minute.' Pooch waved and went out of the door.

I walked over to my mother, and she hugged me.

"Why don't you sit and tell me exactly what happened tonight with Brandon and don't leave anything out. Your father is gone so you don't have to sugar coat it."

"'I'm fine, Mom.'"

"Your father and I are going to take Brandon to see a therapist tomorrow. I want you to tell me whatever you're feeling about what happened tonight. I also want you to let go of whatever it may be and understand that you're not to blame for any of this. Talk to me Mikasa.'

"'I'm fine, Mom, is Dad, okay?'"

"Mikasa please, I apologize for letting Brandon take advantage of you for all these years. I apologize for not shielding you from this and I also apologize for taking you away from your father. Away from his home, his love, you need to be with him. I have to let him do his job from now on. I want you to move in with him tomorrow and stay there until you head off to college. Do you have a problem with that Mikasa?"

"' Not at all Mommy, I love you both and please don't beat yourself up over this. I will gladly go to Daddy's. I know that he's lonely.'" I gave her that look.

"'Am I going to the therapist too?'"

"I would like to take Brandon first just to see where he is at with this without your presence. If you want to come later that is fine but we really need to get to the bottom of this now so talk to me baby."

"'Well, we got to the prom, and everything was fine, but he didn't introduce me as his cousin, he just said this is Mikasa. He held me close during the slow songs but loosened his grip when he saw that I was uncomfortable. After an hour or so we went to the W Hotel when he was bored with the prom and that was fine, but he drank something at the prom before we left that he said was fruit punch, but it wasn't. I smelled it on his breath as he laid his head on my shoulder. He kept complimenting me and saying that he loved me. He seemed to be drunk.

We got to the W, and we were having a nice time stepping, and waltzing and then Always and Forever came on. He held me close, and I rested my head on his shoulder and closed my eyes thinking of you playing the song here at the house and then he felt my butt and kissed me on the lips at the same time.'"

We were on the couch now and Mommy sat back in horror. "What!"

I continued. "'I was momentarily stunned, and I pushed him off me and walked out. He followed and said he was sorry that he thought that I was Kim but then in the same breath he told me to stop tripping because we always kissed when we were little. I remember *him* always kissing me, but I wasn't having this argument on the street, so I waited until we were in the car. We got in the car, and I was really pissed at that point so I said, "Please just take me home so that I can see my man, meaning Pooch. His response to that was that he was my man, and he didn't spend all these years loving and protecting me so that another man could have me.'"

"He said what!" Mommy was pissed now and fuming at this point, but I continued again.

"' I was astonished and figured that he must have had a little X in his drink or something to trip him out. I looked at him and reminded him that we were first cousins, that I was yours and Daddy's' child. I was trying to say things to bring him back to the here and now and then he said that he loved me, and I loved him and that a title shouldn't keep us from being together.'"

Mommy was through.

"' I took off the corsage and the jewelry and tried to give them to him, but he wouldn't take any of it. He said that he was tired of hiding his love for me. And that he showed me tonight that he could take care of me better than any man could even my daddy.

I couldn't take it anymore; I told him not to say another word until my normal cousin returned. I don't know what he was drinking but when he was talking to me, I was convinced that he thought what he was saying to me was the most normal thing in the world. I was disgusted by it and frightened because the boy that I grew up with and loved like a brother didn't love me the same way anymore. I felt like I lost my best friend, and he didn't even understand it. What happened to him, Mom? Why is he acting like this?'"

I laid on my mothers' chest and cried, and she cried. I know now that she didn't ever imagine that it would be this bad.

## PATTI

Mikasa is my daughter and Brandon is my nephew. I love them both, but I hate my nephew right now even though I know that I'm to blame for these feelings that I have. I let Mikasa baby him and I let him sleep with her in her bed when they were little, and I let him kiss and hug her all the time. I thought that it was so innocent then.

They grew up together and both are my world, but I never factored in that his crush wouldn't melt away. I never thought that he would cross that line with his own cousin. I saw all the signs and ignored them. My nephew, my only nephew made moves on my daughter, his own cousin.

Mikasa is crying now and so am I. I'm crying because he hurt her, and I'm also crying over their lost innocence. They are still teenagers, but everything has changed, and I still have to find a way to love him while acknowledging my daughters' loss of innocence forever.

This is going to be harder than I thought, and I really don't know if Darius is going to be able to stomach it, but he has to know.

Mikasa and I sat for about an hour as I comforted her and then I walked her to her bedroom, and she got into bed. It was almost four in the morning, which was too early to call Darius. I would have to tell him before we picked Brandon up later. There would be no more secrets.

## DARIUS (The Father)

'How is my daughter?

Pooch looked at me for a moment and then he responded.

"She seems to be okay. She was really disgusted with Brandon drinking. It's hard to believe that he's only fourteen. How long has he had this crush on Mikasa?"

I shook my head.

'Do not stall Darius. I don't even want to talk about that right now. He is so far beyond the crush phase, and he has been testing my patience for years. Tomorrow we're taking him to a therapist, and I don't want Mikasa to be subjected to any of it. I'm trusting you with Mikasa tomorrow. Anything that she wants to do just let me know and it will be fine. When she calls you later today let her know that you will help her move some of her stuff to my house on Sunday after church. She will be staying with me until she goes away to college.

Brandon isn't going to have the access to her that he had in the past. I'm done playing with him.

Now you say that my daughter is fine, but it feels like there's a lot more going on than I'm being told. Just tell me this, did he touch her last night?'

It was killing me, but I had to maintain Mikasa's' confidence. "Mr. Jones Mikasa told you that she was fine, and it seems as if she is."

'So, you're saying that she didn't tell you different?'

"I'm simply repeating what I heard her tell you and I don't mean to seem elusive but if there is anything else that she wants to tell you I really think you should hear it from her. She won't respect me if I tell you everything, she tells me and if I tell her everything that you tell me you won' respect me. Besides, she loves you too much to keep anything from you for long. You have to trust and believe that sir.'

'Oh, aren't you the clever one?

I'm not going to press you about this because I understand that you don't want to betray my daughter but let's be clear on one thing, Mikasa's' safety is paramount here. If I can trust you, you and I will be running interference with that boy from now on. I don't know what to expect today from him or me, but I do know that he won't be instantly transformed into what I want him to be so this may be more than you signed up for. Where do you stand on this?

"You can trust me Mr. Jones and whatever it takes to make sure that Mikasa is alright is not a problem for me.' I paused for a moment. 'I like her very much; I respect her, and I was completely uncomfortable this morning when she called me and told me that she was going to Brandon's' prom but I held my tongue. I met them at her school this afternoon and he was cool with me and that made me suspicious because it's apparent that he doesn't like me, and he doesn't speak to me, but I decided to be there to sit back and observe. We went to the nail salon and the hair salon, and he paid for everything acting just like a boy in love.

And then came the shoes, the dress, the jewelry.

I was jealous for a moment because I never saw cousins interact with each other that way. And the shoes, everything was so sexy and when he put the diamond necklace on her neck and his hand lingered there, I fought in my head to keep my cool in front of your wife.

And your daughter is so generous, kind and patient with him so it was such a struggle for me not to pull his coat right in front of her because she was still holding on to the memory of the innocent Brandon that she grew up with and he's gone. She didn't see what I saw when I looked at him. He just couldn't keep his hands off her; even in front of me. But anyway, I think that I have said too much already. Whatever you need, Mr. Jones. I will do."

I was pacing the floor again. A boy in love! I shook my head. 'You know, I'm going to share something with you because I normally don't discuss my personal business, especially something like this, but this situation is quite unusual.

I trust that you will keep this between us and only us. I spoke to Brandon's mother this evening after you left. Patti has one sister: Sara with one child,

Brandon. Sara has always resented her parents for favoring Patti. So even though Sara says she loves her sister she's very jealous of Patti and never liked me because I married Patti and her man, Brandon's father, has nothing to do with her.

So, Patti being the sweetheart that she always has been decided that even though we were young and taking care of a two-year-old with her in medical school, she began to keep Sara's baby on the weekends.

Now at that time, I did some things to secure my family's' future and help Sara from time to time and eventually Sara somehow caught wind of what I was doing to supplement our income and told Patti.

Mikasa was five years old at the time and things were going well with all of us even though we had Brandon most of the time, but Patti wouldn't tolerate what I was doing. We went back and forth about it a bit but the result of Sara's revelation to Patti was Patti leaving me and taking the children with her.

Of course, I was devastated but the point of this story is that Sara never took any responsibility for her child and when I called her out on the prom situation she actually said that there was nothing wrong with the crush or her son buying Mikasa whatever he wanted to buy her no matter how expensive. And she leased the Maybach for him. He's fourteen and she has hundreds of thousands of dollars in an account that he can access at his leisure with his debit card, and she's not fazed by any of it. She gives him every material thing that he desires but refuses to parent or nurture him in any way.'

I looked at him with a matching look of disgust on my face. He continued.

'How do you deal with someone like that? Patti considers him to be her son and I must admit that without her I guess he would have been shipped off to his grandparents in Florida, but they don't want to deal with him either because of Sara. This whole situation is messy.'

## BRANDON

My phone was going off again and my head was still pounding. I looked at the clock. 11:30 AM. I picked it up hoping that it was Mikasa.

'Hello, Brandon?'

Good morning, Auntie, how's Mikasa?

'Brandon I'm coming to pick you up in an hour please get dressed.'

Okay Auntie I …

"Brandon we will talk when I pick you up, okay?"

Yes Auntie.

I heard a click, and she was gone.

Memories began to flood my mind again. Mikasa was in my embrace, her eyes were closed, I touched her butt, and I kissed her! Oh no, what have I done!

I got up off the bed trying to get my head to clear. I let the shower run and stepped in. I put my head under the steaming water replaying my aunt's voice in my head. She was not happy.

What will I do now?

## PATTI

I rang the bell. Darius hated it when I rang the bell. I had keys but respected the fact that we were separated for eleven years and that he may have company. We just decided to get back together so you never know what loose ends had to be tied up.

Darius called me at 10AM and I was already awake. He couldn't sleep and of course I couldn't either. I needed to talk to him before we picked up Brandon. He came to the door fully dressed.

'Good morning, Patti.'

"Hey baby."

I hugged him and he let me. When he hugged me, I began to cry. We sat on the couch, and he just held me and let me cry.

'Listen Patti I'm not playing the blame game anymore. We have to be strong, and I'm here for you all the way. You know that don't you? Please don't tell me that something else happened? I know I worked you over emotionally, yesterday in our conversation but I was angry, and I apologize for that.'

"Brandon touched Mikasa's butt and kissed her last night at the W, I blurted out. He also said a lot of foolishness that we don't have time to discuss right now. We have a one thirty appointment, and we really need help to deal with this."

Darius had one fist clenched on his thigh as he wiped my tears with his other hand.

'Come with me Patti.'

He led me to the bathroom, got a cloth and gently wiped my face after dampening the cloth. He surprised me by hugging me and thanked me for telling him. He grabbed his keys, and we headed out the door.

## POOCH

'Good morning Mikasa when you get up give me…

"Pooch, hi how are you", she said, in the midst of stopping the answering machine.

'I didn't want to wake you. How do you feel?"

"I feel all right. What is going on?"

'Your dad told me that you're moving in with him. He wants me to help you get your things over there tomorrow after church. When would you like me to come over?'

"'Let me take a shower and throw something on. How about an hour? I could make some French toast or pancakes if you like.'"

'Why don't you get ready, and I can bring something with me. What type of pancakes do you like? I can stop at the diner.'

"What is the matter? Are you scared to try my pancakes?"

I laughed. 'You will have plenty of opportunities to cook for me. Let me pick something up and you can take your time and bathe. What do you like?'

"I like pancakes with strawberries and cream."

'No omelet?'

"No, I don't have an appetite for that right now but when you get here, I should be a bit hungry so just the pancakes."

'Are you sure that you're, okay?'

"Yes, I will be fine when you arrive."

I smiled and said goodbye.

I went to the storage place on the corner and bought a dozen boxes. I drove over to the diner and picked up our breakfast. I got to the house and

Mikasa opened the door wearing shorts and a Vassar tee shirt. I kissed her lips, and she hugged me. Her hair was all over the place in loose curls, and she looked beautiful.

'You smell delicious.'

She smiled.

"Is that me or the food that you smell?'

'It's you.'

"Thank you. You look nice too."

I just had on jeans and a tee shirt, but I appreciated the compliment.

We went into the dining room and Mikasa had plates, napkins, and silverware on the table along with two glasses of milk and a glass of orange juice. I put the bag on the table, and she asked me to sit. The steaming white towels were at one end of the table near her plate. She dished the pancakes and omelet on a plate for me and put one of her pancakes and some fruit on her dish. She grabbed one hot towel and rested her leg on my thigh as she took my hands one at a time and cleaned them with the towel. She kissed me on the neck, thanked me for breakfast and sat down. She wiped her hand with the other towel then blessed the food. We ate in silence. I watched her try to look as if she didn't have a care in the world.

'What do you want to do today?'

"Wow, I get to choose? You are always so elusive I don't even know what to say right now. Let me think."

I got up to put the plates in the sink and she stopped me.

"You brought the meal so I can handle this." I cleared the plates and containers off the table and washed my hands.

"Thank you so much for bringing the boxes. I'm excited about moving in with my dad, but I think that I will pack everything up tomorrow. I have a feeling that Mommy won't be here when I finish school so I will just move everything over there. I'm hoping that this situation puts my parents back together again.

Why don't we head out to Jersey to Great Adventures I love it there."

'Okay, do you want to go to the water park too? I will have to go by the house and get some extra clothes.'

"Yes, that sounds like fun! Can Jada and your cousin come too?"

'No, they can't. It's just you and me today Mikasa.'

She smiled at me and kissed me. I could taste a mix of Crest and syrup in her mouth and some other sweetness that I couldn't name. We kissed for a while until I stopped her and said, 'let's go to your room.' She smiled but I grabbed the boxes and followed her. I put the boxes in her closet until tomorrow. She put a change of clothes in her Prada backpack and put on her Prada sneakers.

"Let's go. I can't wait to see your place.'

'Let me just run up and grab something right quick. I just spoke to your dad, and he won't appreciate me bringing you upstairs. I will invite you over another time.'

"Are you hiding something or someone? Why can't I come inside?"

'What could I have to hide? You know that your father…

"I will behave myself in your house. I won't take advantage of you. Trust me.'

A big Kool-Aid smile burst across her face, and I couldn't help but smile back at her.

In my mind I pondered over her comment wondering if I could behave myself in my own space.

We left the house and got into the Suburban.

"So, Pooch I'm curious. How many vehicles do you have?"

'Just the Audi and this, I had a motorcycle, but I sold it. And after meeting your father, I'm glad that I did. Can you drive?'

"Of course, but I just signed up officially for lessons last week. Mom thinks that I should learn now even though they won't buy me a car until I'm eighteen. I would like a convertible Caddy, but my dad isn't having it. He's insisting that no one should start out with such an expensive car."

'Convertible Caddy? Isn't that…

"About fifty-five grand used I know. I shop like I have a job. I guess an old convertible Benz could work."

'A Benz for your first car? I guess that could work but why don't you start in the Audi? You know that you could practice in my car if you like.'

"You would let me practice in your Audi?"

'Why wouldn't I Mikasa? It's just a car, and I'm insured. Let me speak to your dad about it and if you're comfortable with that, we could start next week.'

"That would be great! Are you really this nice all the time or will you transform into something else after I fall in love with you?"

'Why would you say that Mikasa? If you're good to me, I will be even better to you and as we get closer and closer there won't be anything that I wouldn't do for you or give to you.'

"So, we're off to a good start, and I know that you're nice. I just said that because I like to hear you speak. Your voice is so comforting and soothing.'

'Thank you Mikasa even though it seems as if you're working me over again.'

I pulled up in front of my house and parked. I went around the car to open her door and escorted her to my front door. We walked into the house and Mikasa looked around admiring the leather furniture, the massive television and all the other furnishings.

"Who decorated this place, I love it! Why didn't you bring me here before?"

'I decorated it. I mean most of the drapes and rugs were chosen by my mother, but the furniture and television and that dining table are new. I bought them about six months ago.'

She stared at a picture of my parents, and I paused.

"They are a good-looking couple. That's why you're so fine. I wish that I could've met them."

'I wish that you did too. They would've loved you. Can I get you something to drink? You can watch television or listen to music while I get ready. The remote is on the end table right there.'

"Can I see your room?"

I knew that was coming. 'Follow me.' I took off my sweaty shirt as she walked around my room. She gasped at the 11x14 picture in the frame on my dresser.

"You just took this picture yesterday didn't you and I look good don't I?"

I laughed.

'I love your modesty Mikasa. Of course, you do. That is one good thing that occurred yesterday. I have a beautiful picture of you now and I can't wait to put some pictures of us up there and in my wallet.'

She hopped on my bed and laid back. I was so glad that I made my bed this morning.

"I usually don't hop on a bed with my street clothes on, but I couldn't resist. A waterbed Pooch. Wow, player, player!"

'Player, player Mikasa, really? A waterbed is just a bed, and my father bought the bed for my sixteenth birthday as a joke because I asked for a car.'

"So did you ever get the car?"

'Yes, I did. I got the bed when I was sixteen and I got a car; a used Lexus when I turned seventeen.'

"So how many girls have been in your waterbed Pooch?"

'Well, I'm nineteen now, one girl a week fifty-two weeks.'

Mikasa pouted and I smiled. 'There was one girl Mikasa; the one that I dated in high school.'

"One girl and you're nineteen? What's wrong with you?'

'What's wrong with me? What's wrong with you Mikasa? Why haven't you done it yet?

Yes, I could do it every night if I wanted to, but I'm very particular about women. How they look, how they act, how they smell, how they taste. When I kiss a girl, I can tell if I want to go further than that. Now what about you? What's wrong with you?'

"Well for one thing I haven't done anything because I fear my Daddy's wrath and the other thing; the main thing is that most boys just turn me off. My parents taught me from day one that nobody has a right to touch me unless I want them to, and they have been instilling that in me for years and it's sticking with me now. Have I been tempted to have sex? Maybe, once, but the way men approach me and try to touch me before they even know my name, which turns me off immediately.

Brandon isn't the only one who can't keep his hands off me. You would be surprised to see how many boys believe that they have a right to touch any girl that they want to. I have had so many arguments with boys at school about respect and my personal space, but they still don't get it."

I listened to Mikasa as I looked through my closet and grabbed two pairs of shorts and two shirts. I took off my socks and I was about to let my jeans drop to the floor when Mikasa took a picture of me on her phone.

'Mikasa! Please delete that. If your father sees you in this house with my shirt off it will be over for us before it starts. Give me that phone!'

I grabbed for her, but she kept on moving away from me.

"You have a picture of me. I need a picture of you. And you look so good too. Look at those abs and pecs!"

'Thanks, Mikasa, but give me that phone please!'

"My father isn't going to see this picture on my phone. Come on Pooch!"

I reached for the phone, and she pulled me on the bed. We kissed for a moment and then I got up off the bed bringing her with me.

'As much as I would love to have you in my bed Mikasa and as nice as you look in it, this isn't happening today. I can control myself outside and in your house, but you're in my house now, my comfort zone and I'm worked up already so you can stay here if you want to but please be easy. You had me going crazy kissing you earlier. Let me change so that we can get out of here. And please delete the picture. We will take some at the park, okay?'

"With your shirt, off?"

'Mikasa!'

She murmured a yes as she deleted the picture. She laid back down on my bed and closed her eyes.

I went into the bathroom and closed my eyes as I washed my face. This was not going to be easy.

## MIKASA

Man. It's going to be a challenge to save it seeing this man. He's so sexy, and his manners and that attitude are turning me on even more. I never ever felt like this before, and it's scaring me to death.

Kissing him is like riding a big wave in the middle of the ocean, it's exciting and dangerous. Each kiss is addictive and satisfying. Once I have one, I want another and another and I have to control myself. Could he be the one and who exactly meets the one when they are only sixteen?

Well, my parents met at sixteen. Actually, Mom was sixteen but what in the world were they thinking? I think that I'll go into the living room now or better yet the kitchen and pour myself a glass of cold water. I'm dying to go into that bathroom right now and mess with him, but I think that I better dial it back a few notches before I get myself in trouble.

I quickly and quietly left his room and went into the kitchen.

After a while I heard his door open, and he was in front of me fully dressed with bag in hand grabbing me to follow him. He locked the door, and we were off to Great Adventures for a day of fun in the sun.

## Chapter 9 – INTERVENTION

I could hear voices outside of my door right before I heard the knock. I put on my socks and my sneakers. I opened my door and was surprised to see my aunt and uncle standing there.

'Hello Brandon, they said in unison without any emotion.'

"Hello. Where are we going and where is Mikasa? Is something wrong?"

My aunt looked at me for a moment and then she spoke.

'Yes, Brandon something is wrong. We are going to a neutral place to discuss what's wrong so that we can get everything out in the open to fix it. We're a family that can no longer hide from its problems.'

Uncle Darius was silent.

"Auntie, what are you talking about?"

'Let's get to our destination and then we will discuss it. I love you and I don't want you to go through this alone. This will help all of us in the long run so just get in the car and sit tight until we get there.'

Uncle Darius drove and we listened to the radio all the way there saying nothing to each other. It felt surreal and I hoped that they weren't taking me to a hospital to have me committed. My uncle pulled off the road and stopped in front of a non-descript gray office building. We exited the car, walked into the building and up to room 1004. A young woman greeted us at the door. She approached me first.

"'Hello, are you Brandon? It's so nice to meet you. Please step into the office on the left. Karen will see you now.'" I was nervous but I proceeded through the doorway.

My Aunt and Uncle were behind me, and we all entered the office and took a seat. The therapist introduced herself and said, ""Hello everyone, since this is your first appointment, I would like to hear from each of you individually and then we can examine the discussion as we go along. I am Karen and you are?""

"I'm Brandon, their nephew."

'I'm Patti Jones.'

""'I'm Darius Jones.'""

""'Okay Patti, may I call you Patti?'""

My aunt said yes.

""'Patti why are you here today?'""

My aunt sighed and said, 'My nephew Brandon is infatuated, I mean he's in love with our daughter. He took her to his prom last night, he touched her butt and kissed her on her lips while she had her eyes closed and was completely unaware of what he was doing to her.'

""'Please continue.'""

'For the last 13 years I've raised Brandon like he was my own son. My sister works all the time and isn't responsible for him in any way besides monetary and he spends most of the time in my home where he has his own room and has been cared for by myself and my daughter for the bulk of his life. Unfortunately, in my desire for them to be like siblings I allowed him to get too close to her. As a child he was very affectionate with the both of us but of course being closer to his age and size he favored my daughter, Mikasa, giving her most of his attention.

My nephew is a popular, handsome all-star basketball player but he chooses to spend all his time in my house running behind his cousin. For his prom he purchased a thousand-dollar pair of shoes, nine thousand dollar; actually, two nine-thousand-dollar dresses to ensure that our daughter, Mikasa, had the proper size dress and twenty-five thousand dollars' worth of diamond jewelry. He also picked her up in a half a million-dollar leased car. In retrospect and hearing myself say this to you I know it must sound very bizarre and out of order for family to do with each other and even though in my mind I knew that everything about the scene that played before my eyes was wrong, I told myself that this is Brandon and it's okay because he is my nephew, we are family.

Please understand that I regret that I let any of it take place. And I'm clear that I must protect my daughter from any person who seeks to harm her, emotionally or physically. Even, and especially if the offender in question is my own flesh and blood.'

The therapist looked at my aunt to make sure that she was finished speaking and then she said, ""Who would like to speak next?""

Darius looked at me and then he spoke.

""As soon as this boy could walk, he chased after my daughter. I tried to tell my wife that boys and girls shouldn't spend all their time together because they need to mingle with their peers, but my wife ignored me because she thought that I was jealous of the attention that she and my daughter gave him. I could see that he had feelings for Mikasa at an early age that weren't natural between cousins.

He was an affectionate boy with Patti, but he would always kiss Mikasa in the mouth until they were about six and eight. I caught him once when Patti wasn't around and told him that if he ever kissed Mikasa on the mouth again I would send him back to his house with his mom for good and I didn't see him do it again. I know that it sounds harsh to say to a five-year-old, but he was so aggressive with her that I thought it was necessary to say it exactly that way so that he would know that I wasn't playing.

Now, I don't know if he actually stopped because he was sneaky when it came to Mikasa, but I didn't see him do it again. He also hugged her up when they were watching movies or playing outside or even just walking around, he would hold on to her. I spoke to Patti repeatedly about it, but it always was ignored. Her nephew could do no wrong in her eyes but now I am at the point where I know that I can't take it anymore doctor. It must stop now for his sake and mine.""

There was another pause and then I spoke.

"I cannot deny that everything that was said here so far is true. It's funny to me that I can remember incidents back that far in my life with Mikasa, but I can, and I apologized to my cousin for touching her butt and kissing her, but I do love her. I love her like my aunt and uncle love one another. Since the moment that I saw her, I have been in love.

She is the most beautiful, the sexiest, the purest girl that I know, and I know a lot of girls. No one makes me feel the way I do when I'm with her. She is the primary reason that I do what I do, as well as I do, which is play ball. Ball players get all the girls' attention and I wanted to guarantee that I had Mikasa's' full attention. Ball players also make a lot of money so I figured that would get Mikasa's attention too and that I could provide for her in the manner to which she is accustomed. I intend on being a professional ball player with my cousin Mikasa as my wife. I….

My uncle got up and came towards me and I covered my throat this time. Aunt Patti held him back, and I continued. But the therapist, Karen interrupted.

'Now can you pause for a minute Brandon? Let's go back to what you just said and why you said it. Are you saying these things to cause a reaction in your uncle, or do you really mean what you are saying? And please Darius I know that this is difficult to hear but try not to react.'

No. I love Mikasa, and I mean every word of it. I have tried for so long to ignore and divert my attention to other girls, but it doesn't work. I play ball Ms. Karen, girls are after me all the time but no one, not one of them makes me feel the way that Mikasa does.

Karen interrupted again.

'Okay so how do you feel about your uncle?'

What does he have to do with this?

My aunt and uncle were extremely uncomfortable now.

'Please answer the question, Brandon.'

Well, my uncle doesn't like me, so I don't particularly like my uncle either. He never liked me even as a child.

Uncle Darius got up again and paced the floor now. My aunts' facial expression was sheer agony. The therapist continued.

'And what about how your aunt feels?'

I have done all that I can to make her proud of me, to show her that I am worthy of Mikasa. I don't know what else to do right now.

'Let me ask you again. Does it bother you that your aunt is unhappy about what you are saying?'

Yes and no. It bothers me that she is unhappy but no; because what about my happiness? All that I have in this world is my aunts' love, Mikasa and my mothers' money. Who is looking out for my happiness here? Who is going to give me what I want?

'But what does Mikasa want?'

She doesn't realize it yet, but she wants me too.

'If Mikasa tells you that she doesn't want you, will you let her go and consider loving yourself, maybe being responsible for your own happiness?'

I don't understand the question.

At this point Darius interrupted.

"Karen, can't you give him some medicine for this? I mean he is clearly unstable. Can we commit him?"

Commit me? You messed up with my aunt and you want to commit me? You blame me for keeping your wife away from you and you want me committed? I'm just a boy.

He lunged at me and now Karen asked him to step out.

Now who needs to be medicated!

That comment disgusted my aunt, and she walked out to console my uncle. I continued.

Now here we are, and I'm alone again. If Mikasa was here I wouldn't be alone. She would console me. I looked at the doctor and she looked back at me expressionless.

## MIKASA

My hair was drenched, my belly was full, and Pooch won a bag of stuffed animals for me. We got on Lightening Loops and Free Fall three times, and also every roller coaster and water ride in both parks. At one point Pooch wanted to go to the safari but I begged out. As we prepared to leave, I pointed to the merry go round and Pooch laughed.

'Okay I will get on all by myself. I let go of his hand, he grabbed my waist and moved to kiss my lips and then I heard someone say, 'Pooch, is that you Pooch?'

We both turned to see a pretty woman watching us. Pooch stood holding me looking at her waiting for her to say something. She didn't say a word, so he said, 'Hello Diane, this is Mikasa my girlfriend. Mikasa, Diane and I went to the same high school. How are you, Diane?'

He continued to hold me as she looked at him longingly as if she expected a hug, kiss, or something but he didn't budge. She said, 'I'm here with my family, and I'm fine. How are your parents doing?'

"They passed away last year. Diane it was nice seeing you, take care of yourself." We began to walk away. He didn't seem to want to talk anymore but it was apparent that she wanted to say more but did not. As we walked off, I could sense that she was still standing there watching us. We got on the line together for the Merry Go Round and Pooch pulled me toward a two-seater.

I want to ride the horse. Pooch smiled with a mischievous look on his face and put his hand up and said, 'I will not touch that comment but you can ride again and get on the horse alright?'

"Boy you're so nasty! What are you thinking right now?"

'I'm sorry! I couldn't help it, the way you said that was so provocative. Forgive me. Come sit with me.'

I walked over to him and sat beside him. So, what happened with you two? Look over there. She's still watching us, and she looks like she still loves you.

'Why would you say that Mikasa, she just said hello and asked about my parents.'

She's watching us and the way she called your name and looked at you. It just felt like something was there.

'Well, I used to date her in high school. She cheated on me during junior year, so I didn't go to the prom. She's the only girl that I had in my waterbed. She always claimed to love me before and after she cheated on me but she slept with me on our first date so there wasn't any love lost there for me. After that I became very selective with women. She continued to call until I changed my number, and I haven't seen her since high school.'

Well, it looks like she still has feelings for you. Are you sure that you're over her?

'Yes, I'm over her. I avoided the prom because I knew that she would show out there and make a scene even though she was wrong. I never loved her Mikasa, but she may have loved me. We had some fun together, but I don't know and actually I don't care if she still loves me. That's why I walked away.'

Well, I hate to say it, but I'm glad that she messed up. You two might have been married by now if you stayed together.

Pooch looked at me and smiled. 'I'm glad too.' He held me like he never wanted to let me go. I felt so safe and secure in his arms. The ride seemed to go on forever and I didn't want it to stop.

After the ride we left the park and headed to my house. As he drove, I laid back and he began to sing. "I'm hoping I can make you mine before another man steals your heart and once that beauty is mine, we will never be apart."

I surprised him and sang along word for word. We harmonized well together. When we arrived at the house Pooch turned off the car and we sat for a moment.

'How do you feel about me getting a place up by your school?'

What do you mean? You're only about an hour away from my school.

'I know but I would like to be close enough to see you during those in between times when you're not studying. And honestly, I just want to be as close as possible. You can eat lunch and dinner with me whenever you want to and well, you can do your laundry and keep some stuff there if you like. And don't worry I will ask your parents first just to make sure they're all right with it. Also, there is the issue with your cousin. If something ever happens, I can't have an hour between me getting to you. Doesn't he know where your college is?'

Are you serious? Will you be able to find a place that quickly? The place that you have now is so nice. Are you willing to leave your waterbed for me? I smirked at him.

'What's the matter Mikasa? Do you think that I'm moving too fast? If this is too serious for you let me know now before I go all in with you, and as far as the waterbed goes if you like I can move it to the new place or get a regular bed I mean you won't be in it anytime soon so it shouldn't make a difference to you.'

I smiled at his comment. "It's not too serious for me because I do like you so much already, but I don't want to interrupt your studies and all the other things that you do. We always talk about me, and I don't want to monopolize all your time with my stuff and my life. I also don't want you to feel like security. You're not responsible for keeping Brandon away from me. I can take care of myself you know."

'I know that you can but right now I take my classes when you are in class, and I'm off for the summer. Next semester I will continue to take early morning classes so that I'm free whenever you are. Now as far as you monopolizing my time, I'm into you girl and want to see you as much as possible whenever and wherever I can. Everything that I do besides school can and will be maneuvered around you and your schedule. And as far as Brandon is concerned, I'm quite sure that you can't handle him in any way shape or form so let me protect you as much as I can.

That's what I'm prepared to do when I'm with someone that means so much to me. I know that you are intelligent and independent but let me be that man for you that you trust to take care of you in every way possible. Give me the space to do that and I won't disappoint you Mikasa.'

Okay, so when do you want to look for this place?

'I could probably find a place tomorrow, but we have two months to search so after I speak to your dad you can come and help me choose a place.'

Tomorrow? Are you serious Darius? So, what if you get a place and we like it up there will we stay? I mean once I have my degrees, we may be so accustomed to the quiet that we won't want to return to the city.

Pooch smiled and looked as if he was pondering over many plans in his mind. 'We will see what happens then Mikasa. If you're thinking about it, it will all work out in the end.'

## DARIUS

Patti, I can't do this. This isn't working for me. I sat and listened to all that I could, but I can't go back in there. What's wrong with that boy?

We were in the room adjacent to the one we left Brandon in and now Patti was crying and snotting all over herself. She was inconsolable and I was livid, but I continued.

Now that we have confirmation directly from his mouth that he loves our daughter the way that we love each other where do we go from here Patti? I can't believe that that boy, your nephew, had the nerve to say that he loves our daughter the way that we love each other!

Patti, Patti!

I could see now that Patti couldn't control herself. She was crying so hard that she could barely breathe, and she couldn't answer. I waited for her to pull herself together. I hated to see her like this, but I couldn't get past the anger that I felt toward her for creating this monster. I told myself and I said to her that I wouldn't blame her for this but this monster that wanted to marry his own cousin was really taking me over the edge.

My heart told me to hold and console my wife, but my ego just wouldn't let me. Finally, she reached out for me and as I wiped her face and embraced her, the doctors' assistant entered the room.

'The doctor would like to continue the session separately with you and your wife here and keep Brandon in the other room. She will be with you shortly.'

I wanted to send Brandon far, far away and end all this foolishness right now but of course I couldn't. Patti's desire for counseling negated any chance of Brandon's disappearance.

Again, I considered walking away from Patti forever but that would also mean walking away from our daughter and I could never do that. I don't know why I expected the beginning of a resolution from a boy who had already successfully crossed the line with my daughter. For more than ten years this boy tested the parameters of their relationship and had finally exploited the weak spot and unwittingly I felt as if my wife had served our daughter to Brandon on a silver platter, and he just couldn't back down from it now even if he tried.

Just as Patti began to compose herself Karen entered the room with a box of tissues.

"Darius if you don't mind, we will continue the session separately with me, you, and your wife. Dr. Brennan, a male therapist has taken over your nephews' session.

I sense a lot of animosity between you and Brandon. And he seems to have a problem with male authority. We need to see if he is capable of conversing with Dr. Brennan without him being antagonistic. Also, he may let down his guard now since he is alone in the session. I know that you are angry but try to understand that he seems to be in a lot of emotional pain. Is it possible for his parents to share a session with him?'

I don't…

Patti interjected. "I will speak to his mother about it, but he doesn't know his father."

"Patti, I think that it would be wise for Dr. Brennan to handle Brandon's sessions from this point. At the end of this session, we will assess his needs, but it seems to be leaning that way. He seems to be accustomed to relating to women and so of course he's more comfortable with them. You know and understand that I'm a non-conventional type of therapist, and it's time to shake things up... I want him to feel a shift and experience a non-judgmental male figure to evaluate him. It would also be immensely helpful if his mother or you could participate with him to ensure his comfort with this process, but I understand if you aren't ready for that at this time."

Karen, I know that it's unrealistic to expect an exact time for his recovery so I would like to get an order of protection against Brandon so that he stays away from Mikasa. Do you think that it will impede his progress here?

Patti stiffened momentarily but said nothing. Karen observed Patti's' reaction.

'Why don't we talk for a bit and then you can decide what to do at the end of our session. Which one of you would like to continue?'

## PATTI

My heart is breaking, and I feel… I hate my nephew right now. My daughter, as his wife? How could he think of such a thing! I trusted him with her and loved him for all these years and he betrayed me. For so many years I fought with my husband over that boy and now everything that Darius said about him is true. How do I love him after this? How can I stop blaming myself? I came here today to try to help my nephew, to salvage our relationship and now I feel as if I'm falling apart.

How could my judgment be so off that I endangered my own child? Why can't my sister love me enough to care for her own son? Why do I always have to be the responsible one? I'm tired. So tired.

I'm a highly successful 34-year-old doctor with a sixteen-year-old daughter starting college at Vassar in two months and today I feel as if my life is over. I'm so tired.

Do you have some medicine for me, doctor? I need to stop this pain in my heart and the pain in my head. How do I go on?

I held Patti's hands now, feeling all the pain that she was feeling. I felt connected to her again.

"We must do this together Patti. You must let me back in your heart and let me share the responsibility of keeping our family together. You must believe that I will do my best to be fair in this situation. You also must understand that because of you I'm enduring this, and I won't blame you for any of this from this point on, so you must stop blaming yourself.

We have to decide together to make every decision based on what is best for Mikasa first. That is our child, Brandon is your nephew. If your sister refuses to care for her son, we have to be strong enough to refuse him so that we can heal as a family.

"Karen, I accept responsibility for my part in what happened here today and regret that I didn't form a relationship with him when he was a child. I believe that things could have been different now.'

"Patti, are you holding back anything else? Is there anything specific that you would like to share?

I hesitated. There were so many thoughts running through my mind that I didn't know where to begin. I sighed then exhaled.

My focus right now is Mikasa. I understand that I can't be responsible for Brandon anymore. I know that we brought him here today but once I drop him off, I would like to cut all ties. I can't see him right now. I don't want to see him anymore.'

There was a long stretch of silence. Then the doctor spoke.

"If you can, try to sleep on that decision. Sometimes anger has us do things that we will regret later. Can I meet you both in a few days? I would like to see the three of you work towards favorable middle ground, but time is necessary to sort things out."

'I will try Karen. I have so much on my plate at work but of course the most important thing to me is my family. We will call you on Monday to make our next appointment once we discuss things further. We all shook hands and exited the office. Brandon was seated in the lobby. He stood and looked at Darius and Darius put his hand on his shoulder and said, 'Let's go son.'

I was shocked and a little disgusted that Darius called him that and Brandon was shocked also but he relaxed and walked out of the door.

We got in the car and drove in silence until Uncle Darius spoke.

'When is your next appointment, Brandon?'

"Tuesday at 3PM."

'Do you need a ride here?'

"No, I'm straight."

They dropped me off and I headed upstairs to call Mikasa. I dialed her number. It went straight to voice mail. It was five o'clock. I didn't realize that we had been there for so long.

I dialed my mother's cell phone and of course it went straight to voice mail. I called Aunt Patti's cell then disconnected the call knowing that she would not answer. I sensed her disdain as she looked at me coming out of the doctor's office. I felt her anger towards me when she said goodbye instead of goodnight when I got out of the car.

It is Saturday and I don't have plans or know what to do with myself now.

## POOCH

It was eleven o'clock when we got to the house and Mikasa was tired. I came around and tried to pick her up, but she laughed and got up from the seat.

'I can walk. You are just too much but I appreciate it. Are you coming in?'

Do you think that your parents are home? Let me call your dad.

'Let's just go inside. If they are you can chill for a while and hang out with me.

She unlocked the door and led me into the house. She put her bag down and called out to her mom. No one answered and the house was dark. We walked to her room and as soon as I stepped in, she began to kiss me so softly that I thought I was dreaming. I stopped her.

Let me use the bathroom Mikasa. I've been holding it for a minute. As I walked down the hall, I looked around to convince myself that her father wasn't in the house. I relieved myself and washed my hands and face before returning to Mikasa.

She changed into pink sweats and a tee and pulled her hair back. She looked fresh and pretty.

I hope that you had fun today. I enjoyed myself as usual.

'You know that I had fun. I like being with you.'

I kissed her. Her phone was going off, so we stopped kissing for a moment.

'Let me see if it's my mom. I hope that everything went all right this afternoon.'

She looked at the phone and put it down. She came back over to me and began to kiss me, but I said, 'You don't want to answer it? I'm not going anywhere. You might as well let those other guys know that you are taken. I smiled.

'It's Brandon again. He keeps calling. There have been six missed calls since five o'clock. I don't want to talk to him yet.'

Do you want me to talk to him?

'No let's just leave it alone until I speak to my parents. I need to know where his head is at before I speak to him.'

She looked troubled but smiled and began to kiss me. I led her out to the living room so that we could be out in the open just in case her dad appeared out of nowhere. I put the television on and continued to kiss her.

She sat on my lap, and I kissed and held her like I couldn't get enough. I pulled her hair out of the clip and caressed her hair and her neck. It felt like we were kissing for hours, and I wanted to touch her all over, but I stopped and got up lifting her off my lap.

'What's wrong Pooch? You taste so good. What happened?

I *want you* so we need to stop.

'But I like kissing you it feels so good, I never felt....

I have something else that you have never felt before either but you; we are not ready for that yet.

Mikasa's' phone went off again and she was a bit agitated but this time she answered.

'Hi Mommy, yes, we're home, and we had a ball at Great Adventures. How's everything?'

"Everything is fine baby did you eat?"

'Yes, I'm still stuffed. I don't want to see food anytime soon. We had burgers, fries, shakes, funnel cakes, cotton candy. We ate a lot of mess. I miss you Mommy, are you going to be home soon?

The comment made her laugh.

"And wouldn't you like to know. How is Pooch and what are you two doing?"

He is fine. We are sitting here watching television and he's leaving at midnight.

"Well, your father and I are at City Island having dinner. So, tell Pooch hello and you two behave."

'Of course, Mom it's me Mikasa.'

"Yes Mikasa, behave. I know that you like that boy."

'I laughed; said I love you then goodbye.

My parents were at City Island. That was a good sign. That's where we always went to eat when they were together, but my mother sounds stressed.'

Try not to worry about it. I'm sure that your dad will tell you all about it when he gets home. Your parents are good people. I'm sure that it will all work out.

I looked at Pooch for a minute and then I smiled. I grabbed his hand and led him to my room, but he paused. Can we kiss some more or are you done with me for the night?'

I stopped her and leaned her against the living room wall. "What did you tell your mother? I said as I kissed her neck. She shuddered and I kissed her neck again and her earlobes.

She told us to behave. She turned to face me and kissed my ear. It tingled, sending sensations down to my toes and elsewhere. I took her hand and led her back to the couch.

"Let's stay out here Mikasa because if we go in your room, I will want to lay you down."

'Okay, so would you like something to drink?'

I smiled. In my mind I saw her in a glass, but I said, 'Sure.'

'Are you hungry?'

I smiled again.

"Mikasa don't be funny. I ate more than you did today, and I can't eat another thing. I said that but had a wicked thought in my mind of something tasty.

'Why are you looking like that? What are you thinking? Ooh, I wish I could read your mind!'

I walked away from him and into the kitchen to get the drinks. I brought out some iced tea and we sat and watched a movie for a while before he got up to leave. It was midnight, Pooch thought, and I didn't want her parents to catch me here after that.

"Mikasa, I will see you in the morning."

And tonight, in your dreams, I replied.

I kissed her and she acted like she didn't want me to go. I felt the same way.

## DARIUS

The circumstances weren't the best, but I couldn't remember when I spent this much time with Patti alone. After dropping Brandon home, we went to City Island and sat by the water for hours in silence. At first Patti was very tense and sat with space between us but after shedding a few tears she moved close and leaned against me. We were both very angry, but anger never put distance between us for long until today. No other woman had hurt me the way that Patti did. I also never loved anyone as much as I loved Patti.

She is my first and only real love. The only woman that I would marry and remained married to, to this day.

'You know that I was so pissed at the moment but thank you for reaching out to Brandon after all that he said today. I wanted to leave him right at the doctor's office and I know that a part of you wanted to do the same, but you took the high road and I love you for that.'

"You're welcome, Patti, but what else could I do? You have always impressed upon me the importance of forgiveness even though you don't practice what you preach."

I ignored his comment and said, 'So what do we do now? If you want to get an order of protection against him, I'm fine with it now.'

"We can discuss practical solutions but earlier today I spoke in anger Patti. Let's see how our new living arrangement works out with Mikasa then we can decide. I'm willing to give him a chance. If he stays away from her school, we won't have to pursue that. You know that I prefer to protect Mikasa myself but if he continues to behave in the same manner, we will get an order of protection."

'So do you really forgive me for this?'

I hugged her and she began to sob. "Please Patti, stop crying. You know that I don't like to see you cry. It seems as if you have been crying all day. We can't change what has happened. We must move forward now." She took some tissue from her purse, and I dabbed at her eyes lightly. I held her face and kissed her near her eyes. I kissed both of her cheeks and then I kissed her lips lightly, barely brushing my lips against hers and she didn't stop me. Then I kissed her repeatedly like I did on our wedding night when she was finally mine and she kissed me back like we had just picked up where we left off eleven years ago. We kissed for about forty-five minutes, waking up parts of me that seemed to be dead for so long and then she asked me again.

'Do you forgive me Darius?'

"Yes, woman I forgive you for this, let's just get it all out there once and for all. I forgive you for leaving me, I forgive you for breaking my heart and I forgive you for taking my daughter away, but I thank you for giving her back to me. I forgive you for keeping yourself away from me where you always belonged, and I forgive you for letting your sister come between us. You know that you said that you would never let anything come between us. But I forgive you. I could never love anyone else the way that I love you Patti and do not start crying again, please!"

She smiled at me like I was all that she could see and then we got up and went into the restaurant to eat. It had been years since we frequented the Lobster House and some things had changed but the menu remained the same. As soon as we sat down Patti went for it.

'I will have a chocolate martini, house salad with raspberry vinaigrette dressing and sautéed lobster tails over couscous.

He will have the house salad, two orders of filet mignon medium well topped with fried onions and garlic, loaded baked potato, broccoli, and a Heineken.' The waiter looked at me and I nodded.

"Well, it is just like old times you are ordering for me again. Are you really ready to come back to me Patti? We can do this every night for the rest of our lives."

'Why don't we wait and see how things will play out. I'm eager to get back with you, but I will keep my place until Mikasa starts classes. I want to keep Brandon away from Mikasa and I'm prepared to do that by staying at my place. If we all go over to your, I mean our house, he will be right there trying to stir stuff up. Let's just stick to the original plan until Mikasa goes away. Then we can discuss getting completely back together.'

Patti?

'Yes Darius.'

Do you love me?

Darius, what does that have to......?

Do you love me?

'Of course, Darius, I never stopped loving you.'

Are you seeing anyone?

'You are around all the time Darius. Have you seen anyone with me?'

Do not sass me woman! Just answer the question.

'No Darius, I'm not seeing anyone. I have had lunch a few times with Dr. Yamada but no I'm not seeing anyone.'

Dr. Yamada? The Japanese doctor, isn't he your boss?

'Yes, he is but he's a man so I just thought that I would put that out there.'

You had lunch with your boss? Are you attracted to him Patti? Is there anything that I should know about him?

'Darius what exactly does this have to do with what we were talking about?'

I sat back and looked at my wife. She is an exceptionally beautiful woman so I should have known that anyone would be attracted to her. Even a Japanese doctor.

I want you back Patti so I need to know if there are any obstacles that will prevent that from happening besides your stubbornness.

Now she sat back and proceeded with her usual stall tactics that kept me on my toes.

'I know that you have not forgotten how instrumental Dr. Yamada was in securing my position as Head of Pediatrics at the early age of thirty. He nominated me and swayed the others to vote in my favor. Whenever there is a need in my unit, he sees to it that it is covered and for the last four years he has been taking me to lunch twice a week to discuss hospital business.'

"I do remember all that Miss Patti, so I will ask you again and if you don't want to answer just say so. Are you attracted to Dr. Yamada? I'm a big boy, and I can take just about anything that you can dish out Patti."

'He's successful, kind and very wealthy but he isn't you and although I toyed with the idea of dating him three years ago when I was very lonely and didn't want anyone that was clingy, I couldn't help but think of you.

You were always around stirring up old feelings so I never could say yes when he asked me out after work hours. I also didn't want to jeopardize my position at the hospital. He made it clear that our professional relationship would remain professional and that our personal relationship would be serious leading to marriage. Considering that I still wore my ring it was easier to tell him that I really wasn't interested since I was hoping to get back with you in the future. So, to answer your question, no I'm not attracted to him. I don't even know how to be with another man Darius.

I'm connected to your spirit, so even if I tried to stay away from you I couldn't. So, you don't have anything to worry about with me. Once we are together you know that it's all about you.

So, what about you? You say that you want me back but who are you seeing?'

"Well, you know that I have a lot of options sexy as I am but right now, I'm only seeing Mikasa and you. You know that I don't date, and I never entertain in our home so there aren't any worries for you either. I love you more now than I did when I met you if that is even possible.

But, wow, you have been having lunch with Dr. Yamada twice a week for the last four years and you are sure that you don't feel anything for him? Can I ask you a serious question?

'Yes.'

If you love me and you haven't been with anyone else for eleven years, why do we have to discuss getting back together once Mikasa starts school?

What exactly is it that is keeping you from me Patti?

The waiter appeared with our meal and began to set all the dishes out on the table. Patti looked at her plate, picked up her utensils and began to eat, feeling the heat of my stare. She smiled and rested her knife and fork on her plate.

'Honestly, I don't know Darius. I guess we should discuss some things as far as your business and assets and figure out what I should do with my place. There are some things to consider. I …

"Patti, I haven't done anything illegal since you left, and I never intend to again. We belong together. If you want to hold on to the house, you can although I never intend on letting you go again. Whatever you need to know about my business and my assets can be discussed once you move back in. If you want us to move to a new place, redecorate this place and make it like new, whatever it is let's just make it happen. Stop stalling me out for no good reason Patti please! You are messing with my health and my mental state."

'Oh, I'm stalling now?' She laughed and started to eat. I watched her and began to eat, wondering what exactly was going through her mind right now.

## BRANDON

I watched television. I played video games. I boiled some franks and ate them and now I was bored with myself. Maybe Auntie has calmed down now; I'm going over there to apologize to Mikasa again and make things right. I put on my sneakers and just as I grabbed my keys, I heard the door open.

'Hey Brandon.'

It was my mother. I couldn't believe that she made it in the house before ten on a Saturday night. I was shocked and even more surprised to find myself hugging her and she hugged me back and I didn't want to let go. After a while my mother spoke.

'How was the prom, Brandon? Did you like the car?'

Aunt Patti called you earlier. "They took me to a therapist. Why did you let her do that? They want you to come to my next session to help fix me!"

'Sit down Brandon and say that again. Let who do what? What did you want me to do? I was at work.'

"You're always at work! Couldn't you take an hour to see what your sister was doing to me? Her husband is trying to get me committed! Does that matter to you Mom?"

'Boy they're not your parents they can't do anything to you, and I will talk to them about taking you there without my permission. What did you do to Mikasa?'

"What do you mean what did I do to Mikasa? You know how I feel about her, and I just can't hide it anymore. I kissed her. And I felt her butt.

'Brandon!'

"I love her. I know that it was wrong to feel her butt but what am I supposed to do with the feelings that I have for her?"

'Aren't you dating someone Brandon? What happened to the girl you said that you were taking to the prom? Does she even exist? You have your

191

choice of girls, why Mikasa?'

"Kim does exist, but I didn't want to take her in the first place. I just asked her to make everybody comfortable with me going to the prom and letting Mikasa teach me how to dance. You and I both know that I can dance but I couldn't say that I didn't have a date, while making it seem so important for me to learn how to dance and then ask Mikasa at the last minute to be my prom date. Aunt Patti would have been suspicious.

And sure, I could have taken any of the girls in the school or on this block, but they are all too fast. Do you know how many girls I could have slept with just by giving them a little attention?

My so-called girlfriend, Kim gave it up the first day that I brought her here and the rest of them would love to get their claws on a future professional baller. I'm not interested in quantity Mom. I have been with Mikasa since I was a baby. I love her, she is the prettiest girl that I know, the most intelligent, her body is nice, and she is so kind and polite. I haven't met anyone else like her and I meet a lot of girls and women all the time."

'But she's your cousin Brandon. It was adorable when you had a crush on her as a little boy but now that you are a big young man it can't continue son. When I spoke to Darius earlier, I argued with him about us loving Mikasa too, that he couldn't keep her all to himself. I told him that the two of us shopping for her should not be a problem. But you can't really expect to date your cousin? You and Mikasa are blood, first cousins! You can't expect her father and my sister to allow that to happen. It's unnatural son. You know that I will back you up in anything but this. What you're speaking of is incest!'

"How is it incest if I love her and want to marry her? I didn't force myself on her Mom I want to share my life with Mikasa."

'Brandon, I know that Aunt Patti practically raised you around Mikasa and you haven't been exposed to enough positive young role models but there are plenty of chaste, beautiful young women for you to meet in this great big world.

Travel and basketball will expose you to all types of girls and all of them will not be fast and nasty. Give yourself a chance. You are only fourteen years old and if you're always up under Mikasa, how do you expect those feelings for her to change so that you can really give some other girls a chance?'

"Did you hear anything that I just said? I don't want any other girls. I will not continue to disappoint myself with girls and women that don't measure up to her. I want her."

'Okay Brandon I'm going to take a shower and talk to you in the morning. Don't go to Patti's house because I don't feel like hearing from her again today. You had your keys in your hand, so my guess is that you were going somewhere. Don't stay out too late and you're welcome for the Maybach. Goodnight son.'

"Goodnight." I grabbed my wallet and slammed the door.

## Chapter 10 – SETTING THINGS STRAIGHT

I was on my third chocolate martini, and I was feeling nice. Darius was trying to look agitated, but it wasn't working. I guess I shouldn't have told him about Dr. Yamada. I took his hand in mine and spoke lovingly to him.

'Okay Darius, you want me, you got me; I'm all for being in a relationship with you again, but I'm staying in my home until we drop Mikasa off at Vassar. Now can you take me home please? I think that I've had enough of everything today.'

"Okay but I have something for you at the house. Let's just stop by and pick it up and then I will take you home.'

I gave him the side eye and said, 'What do you have at the house for me Darius and why didn't you bring it with you?'

"Patti, stop trying to run me. Please remember that I'm the man of the house that you are returning to so get that in check now before you move back in!" He looked me right in the eye, laughed then asked for the check.

As we headed out of the door, I leaned on him for support. I finally agreed to stop by the house, and he softened up a bit. We had been through so much together that it was inevitable that we would reconcile. When we got in the car, I laid my head on his shoulder and told him how I had been feeling for the past few months. When we arrived in front of the house, I kissed him, and he relaxed even more. He helped me out of the car and grabbed his keys. Once we were inside, he sat me on the couch and took off my shoes. He began to rub my feet like he used to when I was an intern at the hospital. I leaned back on the couch to enjoy the massage.

"You still have the prettiest feet that I have ever seen."

He moved up to my legs and I kissed him again. It had been so long since I had touched a man or kissed him that my entire body was throbbing. He held me in his embrace, and I leaned him back on the couch. He teased and caressed me for what seemed like hours, and I couldn't take it anymore. I unbuttoned his shirt, and he stopped me.

"I told you that I had something for you. Give me a moment and I will be right back."

I sat on his couch with my body on fire wondering why he would pause to get my mystery package right at this moment. He finally returned with a box, and he rushed me to open it. I thanked him tried to sit it down so that we could continue but he said, "As soon as you open it, we can continue."

I really wanted to suck my teeth, but I didn't. I picked up the box and lifted the cover and inside was the prettiest sheer peach short nightgown and robe that I had ever seen. I started to speak but he grabbed my hand, lifted me up and carried me to the room with the box on my lap. He sat me on the bed and closed the door telling me to call him when I was ready. I looked around for a moment thinking that this was his plan all along to get me back here and seduce me. I got up from the bed admiring the little lace pieces as I undressed. I looked around the room for a moment and then I decided that it was his turn to wait in agony, so I went in the bathroom and turned on the shower. I wasn't going to put the pretty lingerie on my sweaty body. Now how could he know that I would be ready for him tonight? That man is really something else I swear.

I stepped in the shower and lathered up with his body wash. I closed my eyes as the water pulsated all over my body. I felt as if I were tingling all over with anticipation, but I took my time and lathered up two more times before rinsing off and stepping out of the shower. I grabbed a towel and dried off my body noticing a peach ribbon wrapped around three bottles. I picked the set up and it was body soufflé, light body oil and body spray. I had to smile because some things never changed.

Amidst all his toiletries, shaving cream, cologne, and other items was something that he picked up especially for me. I knew this because it was unopened, and it was his favorite fruity scent of peach. I layered all three on carefully and it smelled incredible. I stepped out into the room, picked up the nightie, and put it on as I called out, 'Come on Darius I am ready.'

He must have been standing by the door because he opened it as soon as the words left my mouth. I lay on the center of the bed feeling so refreshed and relaxed as Darius stood near the door admiring me.

'I know that you're going to come closer than that.'

"Of course, I am but I just have to stand back and admire you for a moment. My, my, my Patti you look so good, and it has been so long!"

'Well thank you. I bet it has been a lot longer for me. Eleven years to be exact and I see that you still like La Perla.

I really like this hot little number that you bought me but how did you know that you were going to get to it tonight? It has been so long Darius. The cream, this nightie, how did you know that I would be receptive to this tonight?'

He watched me as he took off his shirt and sat on the edge of the bed. "I don't know how I knew Patti. Let me be honest and say that whenever I see you, I want it to be that night or the next night. I never accepted our separation so I lived life anticipating your return and now that you are back in my life, I still can't believe how fine you still are, and I really missed buying you these types of gifts.

I bought this for you a couple of months ago and I didn't know when the right time would be for me to give it to you. When you kissed me earlier today, I remembered that I had it and after dinner I just figured that you could appreciate it. I also can't remember the last time that you initiated a kiss. That was another clue for me. I have always been the aggressive one in our relationship, and I would never stop trying with you so here we are."

'Yes, here we are.' I leaned in to kiss him, but he stopped me.

'Patti, you know that I want you, but are you ..............

I put my finger to his lips and then I kissed him. 'I want you too Darius, please I want you. Everything will work out baby just relax and take care of me the way that you used to.'

He started teasing me again, kissing, tasting, and caressing me from head to toe until I couldn't take it anymore and then we made love over and over again. He satisfied every ache and need in my body, and I drifted off to sleep thinking about just how much I really loved my husband and how glad I was to be back in our bed.

# DARIUS

Patti was sound asleep, so I had a moment to reflect on the day. I couldn't believe that the day ended like this. After that counseling session I just knew that I would have to kill that boy but all that I felt after he spoke was intense sorrow. He was scarred much deeper than I imagined, and it seems as though I contributed to his pain.

I discovered today that family means more than Mikasa, Patti and I and as much as I dislike Patti's sister for the way she treated her own son I had to admit to myself that I haven't done much better as the uncle who couldn't be bothered with him. So many people have walked away from him that I don't believe that he can reason anymore, and Patti is washing her hands of him now too.

So much guilt, pain and regret put Patti back in my arms and my life again and even though I'm ecstatic about it I'm still mad at her for holding my happiness hostage for all these years.

Yes, we've been friendly, seeing each other and communicating well all this time but it doesn't change the fact that she robbed me of so much time with her and my daughter. As I laid holding her, working through the pain in my heart, I realized just how much I missed her.

I had a wife so many years ago that I slept with and woke up next to, for five short years and then one morning I didn't have that anymore. I raised our daughter from birth; talking, laughing, and playing with her every day up until the day she took that all away from me.

I watched Mikasa before I went to bed at night, and I saw her every morning when she woke me up or as we sat at the kitchen table eating meals together. I missed having my family with me and now Patti was in my bed bringing more joy to my heart than I thought that it could hold but it's still bittersweet.

I used to feel as if Brandon separated us. I blamed him for my pain because it felt as if he wedged himself between me and my family and now, he has drawn us closer through pain than ever before.

We can't go back and undo anything that was done and unfortunately

Mikasa will have to live with that for the rest of her life, but I've decided today to change the way that I interact with him. If I really expect different results from Brandon, I have to be willing to give him something that he never had to try to squash his feelings for our only child.

I wish that my anger could get his mind completely off Mikasa, but I see now; I recognize that my anger fuels him. If I sow anger, it will only reap disaster and now that I realize what I say to him matters I must respond differently.

After Mikasa was born I really wanted another child. I wanted a son. I really enjoyed being a father and I wanted that again with Patti. She agreed at the time but wanted to wait until she finished medical school and I never let go of that thought and always brought it up when she tried to push Brandon on me.

After I had to move out, I resented our separation, so I made up my mind at the time to ignore the boy. Now I see the cost of my actions. All the time, love, and care that I deposited in Mikasa I could've shared with the boy because love multiplies. I thought it would be unfair to me and Mikasa to share our time with him too. And honestly, I didn't want to love or care for Patti's sisters' child; that was her responsibility. I blamed Sara for our separation and felt that if she didn't tell Patti what I was doing at the time she wouldn't have left me. I took my anger at Brandon's mother out on him every time that I saw him, and it came back to bite me in the butt.

Earlier when Patti was crying and blaming herself, I really felt like crap but hated to admit it to her. My ego prevented me from claiming equal responsibility for what happened, but I must do better now. I'm one man dealing with two young men right now and whether I'm ready or want to, I have to deal with them both responsibly because I said that I wanted a son and more than anything I want things to be right for my daughter, so I believe that I have a job to do now.

Thank God Pooch's parents laid a foundation with him and raised him right, so I don't anticipate any problems with him besides my daughter falling in love with him too soon. And man, my baby is growing up too fast, she always has.

Now on the other hand Brandon is going to cause me to rest on my knees and cry out to God all the time but I guess we will all grow together in this. Something that felt like peace washed over me and I finally began to drift off to sleep holding my first baby tight.

## BRANDON

My legs were cramping up and I thought that he would never leave. I've been crouching behind this bush in the neighbors' yard for over two hours waiting for Pooch to leave Mikasa's house. When I arrived, I saw a truck that I 'd never seen in front of my aunts' place, and I figured that it was his. I also didn't see my aunts' car, so I figured that he and my cousin were inside alone. I looked through the window and I could see them on the couch kissing and my blood boiled.

Mikasa was sitting on his lap and the only thought in my mind was that I wish it were me. I heard someone drive up, so I backed up into the dark space behind the bush to continue to wait him out. I had the spare key in my hand that Aunt Patti kept in a mug in the kitchen. I figured that no one would miss the key and soon I would have my opportunity to see and talk to Mikasa about what happened at the W Hotel the other night.

I heard the door open and finally I saw him walking away from the house towards his SUV. He drove off and I waited to give Mikasa time to shower and get in her bed so that she would be relaxed when I came in the house. I approached the door and turned the key carefully in the lock so that I wouldn't startle her. When I closed the door, the house was quiet. I took off my sneakers and walked towards her room. I could smell her almond cookie body cream from the hallway. The room was cool and peaceful and much to my surprise Mikasa was already sleeping with a smile on her face. I didn't want to wake her, so I decided to slip under her cover and lie beside her for a while.

I took several deep breaths to calm myself down before taking off my t-shirt and jeans and then I slide under the comforter. She was so warm, and she smelled so good that I moved closer to her. Her skin was soft and smooth, and it always felt so good to be near her. There was no place that I would rather be. I had my head on her other pillow, and I was so comfortable and could finally feel my legs again but now I was too excited and Mikasa was stirring.

Damn, I'm too close and now she was mumbling something.

'Pooch?'

I was lying directly behind her now unaware that I was caressing her thigh and now my body was touching hers. I kissed her ear very gently, but she tensed up and moved away abruptly. She turned and saw that it was me.

'Brandon! What are you doing in my bed?!"

She had broken from my embrace and was moving out of the bed and backing away from me as if I had the plague. "Mikasa it's me, Brandon."

'I can see that! What the hell are you doing here in my bed Brandon? Why are you doing this to me?'

She was wrapping herself up in the comforter now hiding her beautiful body away from me.

"Doing what Mikasa? I came to apologize to you for what happened last night. Your parents took me to see a therapist earlier today and I realized that I was wrong. They're helping me to work through this, but I had to see you. I tried to stay away, my mom told me to, but I just didn't know what else to do with myself."

'So, you thought that getting in my bed, rubbing up on me and kissing my ear was your way to apologize to me? You have a room down the hall Brandon. You could have gotten in your bed and spoken to me in the morning.

You have to stop this, Brandon!

We've been so close for so long and you're destroying everything that we had. You've always been like a brother to me and my best friend but after this I will never feel comfortable alone with you again.'

I moved toward her to hug her, but she kept stepping away. "How can you say that Mikasa? I would never hurt you."

'What you are doing now is hurting me. Don't come any closer!'

I kept walking towards her, so she pushed me away.

"I just want to hug you Mikasa. Don't do this to me. You know that I love you, you have nothing to be afraid of with me and please don't say that we

201

can't be alone anymore, we can be alone together. You know that I would never hurt you and I can't love anyone like I love you. I think about you more than I think about myself."

Tears were falling from her eyes now and she was leaving the room. 'If you really thought about me Brandon you wouldn't be here in your drawers with an erection standing in front of me. Can't you see what this is doing to me? I'm going to call Mommy. You can stay in my bed if you want to. I will sleep in my mothers' bed.'

He covered his erection with his hands and continued.

"Wait Mikasa please, you didn't give me a chance to apologize. Come back, sit down, and talk to me and please don't cry. I don't understand why you're so upset about this we used to sleep together all the time. I was in your bed last week and you didn't have a problem with it. Come here and talk to me. I'm your favorite cousin, remember? It's just me and you are here."

I had my arms outstretched to her, but she was pissed now.

'I can't believe that you came here to apologize to me for kissing me and feeling my butt at your prom by taking off your clothes and getting in my bed without me knowing and rubbing and kissing up my ear! You don't see a problem with that Brandon?'

"I don't know ….

'Don't talk, just listen. You're saying that we sleep together all the time, but we haven't slept together for over ten years since we were toddlers! Don't you remember my father pulling you out of my bed and making you sleep in your own room because you would sneak into my bed after I fell asleep? You should remember because you cried! And last week while we were watching movies you fell asleep alone on my bed and I was nice enough to let you stay there. I slept in my mothers' bed that night, so no we don't sleep together all the time; we don't! And you sound crazy saying that. We're cousins!

You always say that I'm your favorite cousin, but favorite cousins don't do this to each other, and you were my favorite cousin for so long Brandon but obviously I'm not yours anymore.

Do you understand that right now you're taking advantage of me? You're trying to use my kindness towards you against me, but I won't let you do that anymore. I'm calling my mother on this so they can deal with it right now. You have to stop doing this to me.'

"What are you saying to me Mikasa; you don't trust me?

Just go ahead and call Aunt Patti and Uncle Darius because they know already. I put it all out there today and why are you saying that I'm taking advantage of you? I'm not interested in taking advantage of you.

I just want us to be together and I understand that we won't be intimate until we are married but I'm prepared to make you, my wife. I told your parents that this afternoon, but I guess that you haven't seen them since our session. They were pissed of course but at least now they know how I feel."

Mikasa stood in the doorway stunned by what I said. She recovered quickly though and tried to reason with me. 'Brandon you're only fourteen years old, and you have a great life ahead of you. Why would you want to stigmatize yourself as the weird boy who's in love with his cousin? Do you know how embarrassing that would be for both of us? You're talking about marriage, and you're only fourteen. There's so much more for you to experience in life before you should even think about marriage.

Basketball is your thing; you're good at it. You need to focus all your energy on that, hang out with the guys on the team and meet people. We're young Brandon, and I don't agree with anything that you're talking about. You and I can't be together, and we definitely can't get married. You can't do this to me. I'm sorry. We have completely different plans. I'm dating Pooch and heading off to college and you, you're smart, handsome and a formidable ball player Brandon. The world is yours, but I'm not. You must learn to have a life away from the Jones household and away from me. Can you understand that?'

I looked at her for a moment taking in everything that she just said. I pondered it but refused to comprehend a future that didn't include Mikasa.

"You know what Mikasa I understand what you're doing and what you're saying but if we aren't together nothing else matters. Basketball, like academics, comes easily to me; I don't have to work at either to be great so you telling me to focus all my energy on something that I have already mastered doesn't make sense to me. You see how well I'm doing with both so why would I stop spending all my time with you? What incentive do I have to focus on things that don't need any more of my attention?

Nothing is suffering in my life except for me because I haven't been able to express my true feelings to you until now and finally, I feel like I'm whole. In fact, I wanted to surprise you, but I may as well tell you now. I'm going to Vassar in two months too. I finished my twelfth-grade studies early and I applied to Vassar after you were accepted. Now we don't have to be apart, and you will learn to love me or at least like me just as much as you like Pooch.

I know that you think that you know what's best for me, but I know that you're best for me so don't worry about trying to reason with me and keep me calm until your parents arrive. I'm calm and perfectly content to wait here and keep my distance from you until they get here."

Mikasa didn't say a word after that. She just stared at me and seemed to be working on another strategy in her head.

"I know that you're angry Mikasa, but time will make that anger and anxiety about us cease and if you join us at the next therapy session you can work through that there. Trust me when I say that everything is going to work out fine between us."

Mikasa shook her head and walked away. She went into her mothers' room, closed the door, and locked it. She dialed her fathers' cell. She was shaking and crying as she left her message. 'Daddy, I need you to come over right now. You and Mommy please come home now. Brandon is here.'

## DARIUS

Patti was sleeping so peacefully that I hesitated to wake her, but we were in this together now, so I caressed her back and spoke softly in her ear.

'Baby you have to get up. Brandon is at the house with Mikasa. She just left a message on my phone, and it sounded like she was crying. You have to get up Baby.'

I passed her the clothes from the chair, and I threw on a sweat suit. I grabbed a cloth from the bathroom and wiped her face. I grabbed her hand, and we were out the door.

It was about 2 AM and it seemed as if the streets were clear, and every light was green. We got to the house in ten minutes flat.

Patti unlocked the door and there was Brandon sitting on the couch drinking chocolate milk and watching television like he didn't have a care in the world.

"Hello Aunt Patti, Uncle Darius. How are you?"

I looked at him as if he had three heads as I called out to Mikasa. I heard the door unlock and she came out of her mothers' room. Her eyes were red from crying, and she fell into my arms. Patti wasted no time getting right in Brandon's' face and said, 'Brandon how did you get in here, and why are you here?'

"Well, I found the spare key in the kitchen last week, so I came by to apologize to Mikasa again." He continued to drink his milk and watch television as if he didn't realize that Patti was angry and just as I was about to speak the doorbell rang.

It was Pooch.

As soon as I opened the door Pooch rushed in and punched Brandon in the jaw. Mikasa grabbed him but I intervened and pulled Pooch towards the bathroom. Mikasa was crying again which caused her mother to cry and they both went to the bathroom to try to calm Pooch down. Brandon lay on the floor with blood coming out of his mouth and when I returned to the living room, he raised himself up on one elbow and said, "I am pressing charges. Did you see him assault me?" He reached for his phone, and I grabbed his arm and knelt on it. He yelled out to Patti, but the door remained closed.

'Why are you here Brandon? We just started therapy today and I agreed to continue to go with you as long as you cooperated. Why are you here?'

He yelled out again. "You're hurting my arm! Oww, get off my arm!"

'I asked you a question. Why are you here?'

I can't control myself and I can't stay away. I love her ….

I put my hand over his bloody mouth to muffle his words.

'Stop saying that! If you expect this to work out, you have to stop saying that crazy stuff! If you're thinking about calling the police on Pooch, I will get an order of protection against you for Mikasa and Patti and you won't be able to come anywhere near either of them. Mikasa will also bring charges for molestation against you for feeling her butt without her permission. It will ruin your life and your basketball career before it starts.

Listen to what I'm saying to you! I'm going to move my hand and you're going to act like you have some sense.'

"But I ……..

'Brandon!'

He was silent so I lifted him from the floor and brought him into the kitchen to wipe his mouth and get some ice. I sat him down at the table and spoke.

'Now I'm going to ask you again and I expect a sensible answer. Why are you here and what did you do to make Mikasa cry?

He looked at me like I was crazy and said nothing. I stood directly in front of him.

'Brandon!'

"I got in her bed while she was sleeping, embraced her and kissed her ear. I told her what I said earlier in therapy. I told her that we would be together. I told her that I was going to Vassar."

I rubbed my hands together to keep myself from putting his head through the wall.

'Let's take a walk outside for a minute.' He hesitated of course thinking that I would hurt him. I said it again and he rose to his feet and put on his sneakers. I called out to Patti, and she came out. 'Patti, we're going for a walk. We will be right back.'

Patti glanced at Brandon then turned and went back down the hall without saying a word. Brandon stood still, shocked that she didn't say anything to him. We stepped outside and began to walk.

'Listen Brandon, stop putting yourself in situations where you can't control yourself and stop touching Mikasa!

Tell me, why would you sneak into the house with a key that you aren't supposed to have knowing that she is alone, and you can't control yourself? You know that you didn't come here just to apologize. Why are you doing this to yourself and Mikasa? I could really hurt you right now!'

"I apologize, Uncle Darius honestly, I just wanted to be near her. Whenever I feel like I want to see Mikasa I just get up and come over. I've always done that. After all that happened today, I felt disconnected, and I didn't like the feeling so I had to see the one person that I knew would make me feel better. I really didn't mean to get in her bed. I just came to talk."

'Brandon what you say and what you do are in conflict, and I can only take so much from you in one day. You need to understand that I won't allow you to continue to entertain a relationship with our daughter. It can't happen. We don't want to push you away, but you're leaving me without many options here. If you can't control yourself around Mikasa you can't be with her alone. Do you understand?'

"I hear you but what ......

Do you understand me, Brandon! I'm not asking you I am telling you.

Some things are nonnegotiable, and I refuse to have this conversation with you every day. This is difficult enough to deal with in addition to trying to treat you like my nephew after all this time but don't test my patience. I'm willing to help you through this, but you have to dial this thing back that you've let take control of you. Every time you think, you can't just do. You have to stop and think about the outcome of things before you do them. You have to dial your emotions down to zero so that eventually you won't feel anything when you think about Mikasa.

I know that you think that you're entitled to everything that you see but I'm going to show you another way to live now. I'm going to show you some things, you will start getting out and seeing other people, I will be at your games, we will go to therapy a couple of times a week and you will be accountable for your actions. We will have sessions with Mikasa, and you will respect her space.

I know that you graduate next year so I guess that it may be okay for you to go to Vassar too depending on how things are coming along by that time, but you will have your own life, Brandon. We don't want to send you away, so you have to learn to live by some rules here and we start this today. Why don't you......

He interrupted me and said, "But Uncle Darius my studies are complete, and I begin Vassar when Mikasa does in a couple of months. I wanted to surprise her and just be there when she got there but I guess you should know now. I completed all the eleventh-grade course work and half of twelfth grade in December. I plan to pursue my bachelor's degree before playing for a college team so I figured that I would go to Vassar also. Now if you are saying that I can't go to Vassar now and Mikasa and I can't be together then I don't really care about basketball anymore. What's the point?

Mikasa has always loved that about me. She is my biggest supporter and if she isn't in my corner why should I pursue it? And as far as my feelings are concerned, I can't just change the way that I feel and be 'normal' because you're threatening to send me away. And send me away where? Nobody wants me anyway so where would you send me? You know as well as I do that my grandparents don't want me either. Please tell me, who else do I have in this world and just how am I supposed to change how I feel after all these years?"

I tried to absorb all of what he said but I was stuck on him completing twelfth grade already. 'You must be kidding me, Brandon! What do you mean you finished your studies? You're only fourteen. Are you some type of genius too; and when did you get accepted to Vassar?

"I applied when Mikasa got accepted. I wanted to wait and see where she decided to go before I applied anywhere. I was determined to go wherever she went regardless of all the interest that I received from the top basketball schools. Duke was coming at me hard but since I lacked interest, they backed off pursuing some of the other hopefuls figuring that it would lure me in.

With all these life decisions I'm making it's funny because I'm struggling with conflicting feelings about Mikasa right now. You know how much I love her, but I feel jealous of her too. I mean everything falls in place for her and everyone who meets her likes her or wants to be her. She has Aunt Patti and you caring for and catering to her, Pooch is trying to take her away from me and no one is at all concerned about me and what I need.

I don't know how to deal with all of this. I tried to talk to my mother about it, but she wasn't trying to hear what I had to say. I came here to try to reason with my aunt and found Mikasa here with Pooch. I could see them through the window; I saw how she looked at him. I want that with her. I don't want to be pushed aside I ..........

He held his head in his hands and sat down on the bench. Just as I was about to tell him a thing or two, he started to moan as if he was in terrible pain.

'Son, please. Let's just try to take this one day at a time. We have an appointment on Monday. The four of us will sit down and talk. He was still moaning. 'Brandon, stop it and listen to me. Listen. Do you want us to do this as a family or do you want to go alone?'

He moved his hands and placed them in his lap. He looked at me. His eyes were wet, and it went against everything that I was feeling but I grabbed him and held his neck trying to comfort him. He stiffened and pulled back at first but then he just moaned and let me hold him. The sound that came out of him was beastly, he was almost as tall as me and I felt uncomfortable holding him, but he needed to feel as if someone cared about him. I held his neck for another moment as his shoulders drooped and then I spoke.

'Listen I know that it hasn't been easy for you being an only child without much support from your parents, but you have to be open to this process and understand that there will be times when your aunt and I will be angry with you like we both are right now. You will also be angry with us but all of us have to get our feelings out no matter how painful it will be.

We will work on your mother and try to get her into the sessions as well. I will talk to Pooch about what just happened, but you have to stay away from Mikasa when you know that she's alone. You also must give her a chance to process all of this. This isn't easy for her at all. She loves you. Not the way you would like her to, but she loves you and now she doesn't trust you and I can't say if she will again. Keep your distance from her until she feels comfortable and eventually if you ease up and back off, we will be able to behave like a family.

I know that you're young and impatient and expect everything to happen right away, but you have to learn to be patient and control yourself and we both know that you can do that. We're not enemies Brandon and believe it or not I do want you to succeed in all areas of your life at everything. I want you to date and I want you to be successful, own businesses, get married and have children someday. Anything is possible for you if you just listen, learn, and embrace this process.'

"I am listening to everything that you're saying, and I understand but do you really think that I can just turn my feelings off and on like a faucet? I've been struggling for so many years with this and I can't…….

'Brandon, I know that I will have to let you speak your mind and the majority of what you have to say will make me extremely uncomfortable, but you have to decide to choose your family over your feelings. It won't be easy, but you can, and you will change the way that you feel about Mikasa. A romantic relationship between the two of you isn't happening and the sooner that you grasp that then you will see what's possible when you change your mind set regarding my daughter.

We will get through this and this weekend you and I will head out to Duke to tour the campus. Duke is your best choice for your academic and professional future, but we can also explore other options together. You can't go to Vassar, at least not this year. We have to see how things progress before you're back in Mikasa's presence, and you really need to have a life away from Mikasa anyway and college is a good place to start. I know that it seems unfair, but you have to work with me. I'm doing something right now with you that I never thought that I could do.

 So let me take you home and give your aunt and Mikasa some time to talk and get over their anger about what you just did. After service in the morning, I will swing by and pick you up so that the four of us can discuss what you did. Don' come to church because we need some time apart, but I will call you and pick you up at about 3pm. Patti and I have to work some things out before we see you.'

Brandon was despondent but less resistant to me and he didn't seem to want to leave even though he had worn out his welcome. I decided to take him home because it would be impossible to accomplish anything at the Jones house with emotions running as high as they were. We walked over to my car, got in and headed to his house.

## POOCH

Mikasa and I were still in the bathroom when her father returned. Her mother left the bathroom as soon as she could see that I was calm, and she calmed down also. Tears had been streaming down Mikasa's cheeks non-stop ever since we entered the bathroom and I felt bad because I didn't listen to her. When I answered the phone, heard how upset she was, and she told me what her cousin had done I couldn't think straight. I was really fed up with everything that he had done and was tired of hearing excuses. My anger got the best of me, and I really wanted to beat him until he was completely knocked out, but Mikasa and her father were on me before I could get another swing in.

'I don't know where your dad is with this Mikasa, but I'm not done reasoning with your cousin. I must see him on this, or it will just continue. We all understand that therapy can't reverse his behavior overnight and I refuse to stand by and just let him do whatever he wants to Mikasa whenever he feels like it.'

As I held Mikasa in my arms my blood was boiling. She stopped crying, I kissed her face gently, wet a cloth, wiped her face, and just held her close. Just as she was about to speak her father called out to her.

"Baby girl please come out here and let me see you, you too Pooch."

I hugged her and followed her out of the bathroom. He stood and held out his arms to Mikasa as we approached him. I sat beside her mother on the couch, as he held her for a while apologizing to her and rubbing her arms. He walked her to the kitchen, and they spoke for a while. He spoke very softly to her and then they returned to us and sat down. He glanced at all of us and spoke.

'I took Brandon home so that we could all talk and try to recover from what just happened. Pooch, I know that you're angry, and you feel like you would if any other man put his hands on Mikasa. I also know that you want to serious harm to him, and I feel every bit of where you're at right now and then some. I would never let anyone hurt my wife or my daughter, there's not any question about it, but we're dealing with something here that I never imagined that I would have to deal with in all my years on this earth.

I know about crushes and infatuation. That is how it all started with Patti and I but obviously, Patti and I aren't related and this situation with Patti's nephew being attracted to his own cousin must be handled in a certain way for all of us to be able to live with ourselves.

Think about it for just a minute. And believe me, it goes against everything within me, and I'm sure within you also but if you or I do what we want to do to Brandon Patti and Mikasa will feel a way and Patti's sister will know that it was one of us who did it and will never stop accusing us of it for the rest of our lives. On the other hand, if we abandon him completely and decide that it's not our problem, which it clearly has to be, his behavior will worsen, and we will have to get an order of protection against him which can work for or against us. It will be messy and counterproductive and Patti and Mikasa will still be constantly stressed about that. Mikasa and Patti will feel guilt and regret because of the deep emotions involved here. So as much as I hate to, I'm putting my feelings aside and trying to work with Brandon to get him through this. I also need to keep him close to gauge his progress or lack thereof. He's too smart and cunning to just be left alone.

Now unfortunately, there's more and none of you know this, but Brandon just told me that he completed his high school studies and is planning to attend Vassar with Mikasa this year. He wanted to surprise her by being there when she got there. He said that he was accepted already and planned to register for classes next week based on Mikasa's choices. He was prepared to get a degree alongside Mikasa and then pursue his basketball career and attend Duke once he turned eighteen."

Everyone was stunned and speechless at the revelation except for Mikasa. I continued, "I explained to him that he had to do something to change these feelings that he has for Mikasa and that I would do all that I could to get us through this because I knew that you wouldn't deal with him right now Patti, and of course I don't expect you to, but someone had to. I feel like the only way to beat him at his own game is to play him close and finally get to know him. We will have a group therapy session for just the four of us tomorrow and Mikasa it's time for you to participate. I'm so proud that you finally stood up to him tonight to protect yourself and you will have to be strong and continue to express exactly how you feel, and you will tell him what behavior you will accept. Boundaries would be established, and he would have to adhere to them. You know now that you can't baby him anymore. He's too big and strong for that. We're family but you're going to have to start treating him like a stranger in terms of your comfort level with him. I know that you wouldn't allow any other boy to do the things that he has gotten away with, so you and I are going to work on detaching yourself emotionally from Cousin Brandon. If you see him for what he really is; that is a young man trying to take advantage of you, there will be no choice but for you to react defensively to protect yourself.

I say all this to you baby girl because I'm your father, I love you Mikasa, you know that I do, and I want to make it crystal clear that you aren't to blame for any of this but unfortunately, we all must accept responsibility for how we will respond to Brandon moving forward.

Patti finally said, "'Can't we just ask the doctor to medicate him and get the order of protection? I don't want to deal with him after this incident Darius! He climbed into bed with my baby! I trusted him and this is how he treats me and my baby girl?

I did everything for that boy! I fed him, bathed him, burped him, and stayed up with him when he was sick. I sacrificed so much for him and when Sara was acting out and my parents refused to raise him, I took him in, and this is what he does to me!'" Patti burst into tears, and Darius went to her side to comfort her.

"Patti baby come with me. Let me talk to you in private for a moment.

Give us a moment and we will be right back." Darius took her to her room leaving Mikasa and I at the table.

"'' Pooch, I don't understand why this is happening. Do you see what this is doing to my mother? I always thought that Brandon and I had a great relationship. I shared everything with him, and he was the best of both worlds for me because he was like having a sister to play girl games with and a protective brother figure if you know what I mean. We entertained each other all the time as kids. We would play tea party, Barbie and GI Joe, board games, Tag, and all other kinds of games in the park. He even played Double Dutch and Hopscotch with me. Boys teased him about it, but he didn't care. He was my best friend in the world and now I must treat him like a stranger. Why has it come to this? What was he thinking?"'"

Mikasa shook her head and paced back and forth. I was still reeling over the fact that he was already setting himself up at Vassar. I was so heated, but I fought to stay focused on what Mikasa was saying and feeling right now. I was here to comfort her and make her feel protected. I wanted her to trust that I would always be there for her.

'Mikasa, I know that this isn't easy for you because you love Brandon so much, but he betrayed your trust and only time and distance will heal that. You're missing what you two once had but right now I want you to know that whatever you used to do with him you can do with me and whenever you need to talk about him you can talk to me. I will do everything in my power to make this easier for you and it will feel strange for a while, but we will get through this together.'

When Mikasa's parents returned to the room I was holding their daughter's face in my hand, and she was smiling. It was the first smile that they saw on her face in a while. Darius looked at us for a moment like he sensed that we were getting closer to one another than he liked. It hadn't been long, but we seemed to get each other already and sense things about one another that would have been cool and taken for granted if I were his son. But I was auditioning to be his son, so it made the situation precarious and wrought with emotion. I sighed at his trepidation, and he sighed at what I imagined was inevitable.

I hugged Mikasa and sat back.

"'Mikasa, I need to apologize to you for that outburst. I'm so sorry that this happened. This isn't about me or what he did to me, it's about him betraying your trust and taking advantage of you and we're going to make this right no matter how long it takes. You know when I gave birth to you, I felt like I would kill anyone who ever tried to harm you and when Pooch hit him, I really wanted him to keep hitting him so that I didn't have to. At that very moment I wanted to really hurt him, and I had the most horrible thought in my mind of how to do it. It bothers me to say something like that but there's not anyone on this earth that I love more than you and I take my job of protecting you very seriously. You're my only child, and I will never allow anyone to harm or change you. Your father and I have set aside our differences, and we will all work together and grow from this. Later today after the service your father will get Brandon and the five of us will talk about what happened. Pooch you are welcome to come if you can compose yourself. I will be fighting to compose myself too so I will understand if you don't want to join us but if you do, we will get through the struggle together. We want to include you because Mikasa called you and you got involved but you need to know upfront that you may hear things that defy logic and will absolutely infuriate you. You can decide what you want to do after service, but we all need to get some sleep. Is there anything that you want to say before you go?"'

'If Mikasa is comfortable with me taking part, I will be here later. Please believe that I didn't expect to react the way that I did but when I heard Mikasa's voice, and she told me what happened I felt responsible and I wanted to make her problem go away, but moving forward I will do my best to maintain my composure and thank you for including me despite what happened here. You know that there isn't anything that I wouldn't do to protect your daughter.'

"We understand Pooch. We all want to protect Mikasa but now she must learn how to protect herself too and trust her instincts when it comes to Brandon. We have done enough talking for now and have to be at service in about seven hours so let's get some sleep and meet back here in the morning."

I stood up and said, "Goodnight, ladies,' Darius, and was out the door. Mikasa sighed, kissed her parents, and said goodnight. Darius touched Patti's arm and prepared to head out of the door. Patti held her hand on her husband's arm and said,

"'Do you want to stay? I know that you're tired."'

"Oh, I want to, but I can't wear this to church. It's four o'clock now and the service starts at eleven. Let me get some sleep and I will be back at ten." Darius pecked his wife on the lips and was out the door.

Patti whispered, "I love you Darius," and he was right outside of the door, so he heard her.

"I love you too woman," he replied and then he was gone.

## BRANDON

When I got into my house it was so quiet but the thoughts in my head were loud. I wanted to go back to Mikasa and make her talk to me. She had to see me differently. She needed to know that I was grown, graduated, ready to face the world with her; ready to hang with her at Vassar and challenge and stimulate her mind like I always had. We experienced all our major life changes and growth together. How could she ever manage without me? How would I manage without her?

I felt my swollen jaw and I couldn't believe that Pooch hit me, but could I blame him? He must feel what's going on between Mikasa and I and realize that he can't separate us, and that his days are numbered.

He was threatened by me; a fourteen-year-old boy in a man's body. I had to intimidate him; my size, my skills, my looks, intelligence, my money, and my ability to manipulate any situation that I found myself in.

He could never compete with this, so he had no choice but to hit me. Eventually he had to give up and then Mikasa would be mine and my aunt and uncle would step out of the way too.

I was in the shower trying to control the part of me that got me in trouble with Mikasa earlier and I was at the point where nothing else would satisfy me but her. My uncle was ordering me to dial it down like I could, but he will see that there is nothing that I could do about this love that I felt for his daughter.

I was worked up and tired, so I stepped out of the shower, dried myself off and went to my bed and got in it but how was I supposed to sleep now?

 I thought for a minute and remembered that my mother had some Grey Goose and Hennessy in the bar. Maybe if I sip something then I can mellow out and get to sleep. My mother had so much alcohol in here that she will never know the difference. I liked how I felt at the prom, and I wanted to feel like that again.

That sweet stuff was good but hmm, this stuff here is smooth even though it is burning my chest.

I walked back to my room, steadily sipping. It burned at first but now I just feel nice. The tension across my back began to ease and I felt different. I downed what was left in the glass and laid back. Before long I felt myself slipping off to sleep.

## SARA

'Good morning, Sara.'

"Who is this and why are you calling me so early on a Sunday?"

'It's your sister, Patti.'

"What's up Patti?"

'I wanted to say hello to you before I headed out to service.'

"I guess my son is there with you. What happened now?"

'No, he isn't here. He should be home with you. Can we meet tomorrow for lunch, my treat?'

"It seems like you only call me when he's over there aggravating Mikasa. Is that what you want to talk about at lunch? Is that why you're treating for lunch Dr. Jones?"

'In case you've forgotten you're my sister Sara. I shouldn't need a reason to eat with you. Can you meet me at Breton's at eleven thirty? You have to eat lunch so it may as well be with me tomorrow.'

"What is it regarding Patti? Are you going to grill me about your nephew?"

'Come on Sara can't I just see my sister and take her to lunch? I'm coming to your side of town so can't you be nice for a change and just say yes?'

"Be nice for a change, what are you saying?"

'Sara, my goodness, why do I have to beg you for a lousy lunch date!'

"So now I am a lousy lunch date?"

I was through so I just hung up. It was Sunday and I wasn't going to let her take me there right before service. I would deal with her later. I don't know why I had to have a sister from hell. Forgive me Father, I know that you don't give anyone more than they can handle but that one there always hits every nerve that I have when I speak to her.

I sat up in my bed now cursing at the phone. Then I started laughing to myself because it was so easy to anger my sister. Then I got angry again.

"Oh no she didn't just hang up on me," she said as she dialed her sister, and it went straight to voice mail. She dialed again wanting to curse her out and got voice mail again. She hung up, sipped the leftover Chardonnay on her nightstand and turned over to go back to sleep.

An hour later, deep in slumber I began to toss and turn in turmoil over the discussion that I had with Patti. I began to remember all of my exchanges with her throughout the year and how I spent most of our teenage years antagonizing her. I also thought about the times that I thought I caught our mom scowling and us when she thought I wasn't looking. I remembered our dad apologizing to mom anytime he bought anything just for me. I tossed and turned for what seemed like hours with thoughts of inadequacy, doubt, and anger over how I felt I was treated all of my life. I saw Brandon's father from a distance walking towards me with a frown on his face. I saw Patti and Darius kissing in her room when our parents weren't home, and I wanted what they had. I thought about all the boys that I slept with in high school trying to get what Patti had. I thought of all the time I wasted pushing my sister and son away. I tossed and turned, I sweated and threw the covers from my body but couldn't seem to wake up from this flurry of awful memories.

I couldn't understand why this was happening to me and I needed to wake up to figure out how to change.

## ABOUT THE AUTHOR

Cocoa Brown was born and raised in Bronx, New York.

www.ingramcontent.com/pod-product-compliance
Lightning Source LLC
Chambersburg PA
CBHW060323260626
47160CB00007B/2661